A NOVEL

Last Words

A NOVEL

Last Words

LEANNE BAUGH

Red Deer Press

Published in the United States in 2020

Published in Canada by Red Deer Press,
195 Allstate Parkway, Markham, ON   L3R 4T8

Published in the United States by Red Deer Press,
311 Washington Street, Brighton, MA 02135

Library and Archives Canada Cataloguing in Publication

Title: Last words / Leanne Baugh.
Names: Baugh, Leanne, 1959- author.
Identifiers: Canadiana 20190156120 | ISBN 9780889955769 (softcover)
Classification: LCC PS8603.A8977 L37 2019 | DDC jC813/.6—dc23

Publisher Cataloging-in-Publication Data (U.S.)

Names: Baugh, Leanne, author.
Title: Last Words / Leanne Baugh.
Description: Markham, Ontario : Fitzhenry and Whiteside, 2019. | Summary:
"This profound young adult novel is rich in diverse characters that illustrate what
it is to live fully in this world"-- Provided by publisher.
Identifiers: ISBN 978-0-88995-576-9 (paperback)
Subjects: LCSH: Suicide – Juvenile fiction. | Adulthood – Juvenile fiction. | BISAC:
YOUNG ADULT FICTION / Social Themes / Suicide.
Classification: LCC PZ7.B384La | DDC [F] – dc23

10 9 8 7 6 5 4 3 2 1

Red Deer Press acknowledges with thanks the Canada Council for the Arts and the Ontario Arts Council
for their support of our publishing program. We acknowledge the financial support of the Government
of Canada through the Canada Book Fund (CBF) for our publishing activities.

Edited for the Press by Peter Carver
Text and cover design by Tanya Montini
Printed in Canada by Houghton Boston

www.reddeerpress.com

For Brenda

Life is a spell so exquisite

that everything conspires

to break it.

~ Emily Dickinson

Chapter 1

You walk toward me on the bridge. The summer sun shines on you like a spotlight.

Cars whoosh by.

I hop off my bike. Lean it against the railing. The North Shore Mountains tower behind. I reach into my backpack for my phone. Launch the camera app and zoom in on you. Your square jaw makes you look strong—like Captain America or Thor. I take your photo. Then another.

You're talking on your cellphone. The person on the other end must have said something funny, because all of a sudden you're splitting a gut laughing. So loud, the man in a brown suit who just walked past turns around to see what's so funny. You stop.

I pretend to take a picture of a tugboat pulling a barge, but instead take one of you staring into the Burrard Inlet like you're waiting for a whale to breach. I walk closer.

You turn and look at me with dark blue eyes. Hand me your cellphone.

I think you want me to take your picture.

But all you say is, "I'm sorry." Hoist yourself up on the railing.

What? I reach out my hand. Wait. Wait. My fingertips brush your white shirt before it puffs up like a parachute. I peer down into the water, but only see a log carried by gentle currents.

Chapter 2

Everything's fuzzy. Like taking the glasses off in a 3-D movie. The man in the brown suit is now beside me. His nose hooks at the end like a bird's beak. He doesn't say a word—just grips the railing, staring into the water.

Sirens. Police cruisers pull up. Stop traffic. How much time has gone by?

A woman cop comes up to me with a notebook flipped open. Her lips are moving, but I can't make out what she's saying. Did she ask my name?

I say, "Claire Louise Winters." A warm salty breeze makes my sweaty skin tingle.

The sun sinks lower in the sky, almost touching the mountains. Another cop is speaking to the brown suit.

The cop says something.

"Pardon?" I say.

She hands me her card—Constable Pauline Leong—with all her coordinates.

My eyes blur. Is that her name? I stuff the card into my shorts pocket.

"Your age?"

"Sixteen." Red lights from police cruisers flash in my eyes. I look down and see rescue boats searching the water far below. To steady myself, I rest my hand on my bike that leans against the railing beside me.

Phone numbers—mine and my parents'. My brain is all wonky and I switch the numbers around. Hand her my cellphone so she can check.

"Can you tell me what happened?" the cop asks.

"I was ... well ... first of all ... I was at home."

She nods.

"Then I ... I was biking to North Van ... to see 'Gyre.'"

"Gyre?"

"Garbage ... an art exhibit about garbage ... all the garbage that fills our oceans." I look down into the inlet and my wonky brain imagines the rescue boats stuck in a huge mass of plastic bags, bottles, toys, and fishing nets.

"Go on."

"And I ... And I ..." My brain is mashed potatoes and my tongue feels like it's tied in a knot.

"Take your time." The cop puts her hand on my shoulder.

"I was walking this way ..." I point toward the North Shore. "He came toward me. And then he ... he stopped."

Her hand slips off my shoulder and she starts writing again in her notepad.

"Was he a friend of yours?"

I shake my head. Was? Does that mean he's dead? I feel woozy. With my back pressed against the railing, I sink down to the sidewalk.

The cop kneels beside me. Asks if I'm all right.

I nod.

"You never saw him before?"

I shake my head again.

"Was he acting strangely? Talking to himself or pacing ..."

I shake my head.

"Did he say anything to you?"

My head starts to pound. "He said, 'I'm sorry.'"

"That's it? That's all he said to you?" The cop's forehead wrinkles in confusion.

I nod.

"Any idea what he meant by that?"

I shrug. She looks like she doesn't believe me.

"Go on," she says.

"And then he ... he climbed over the railing." I feel like I'm going to puke.

"Anything else you can tell me?"

I shake my head. *Don't tell her that I reached for him. That my fingertips touched his white shirt.*

The cop studies me for a moment, then flips her notebook closed. "I'll drive you home."

I sit in the passenger seat of the cruiser. As we drive through Stanley Park, I lean my head on the headrest, feel the cool leather, and watch shards of light flash through the ancient trees. I dig my fingernails into my palms to try to stop the prickly feeling. Garbled messages, like the sound of crunching potato chips, blare on the police radio. Cars move along West Georgia Street, head for downtown in fits and starts. Horns honk. Tires screech. Motorbikes rev. In the opposite lane, a fire truck and ambulance whizz by with sirens moaning, heading for the Lions Gate Bridge. Heading for the jumper. When the traffic slows to a crawl and then a stop, people glance over. Do they see me through the window? Think that I'm a runaway, or a criminal?

I feel the outline of my phone in my pack. The photos race through my mind: him walking ... laughing ... peering over the railing ...

I shiver.

The cop looks over at me. "Doing okay?"

I nod.

She looks small for a police officer. I have a hard time imagining her wrestling a biker or a drug dealer to the ground. But the gun bulging out of her holster looks pretty convincing.

We stop at a red light at Pacific Street. A woman with a red floppy sunhat walks on the Burrard Bridge. She stops and looks down into the water. Her fingers grip the railing. My heart pounds so hard I can feel my pulse in my ears. Bubbles of sweat like blisters pop out around my mouth. I lick my salty lips. Close my eyes tightly—my head spins, stomach rolls, as we drive over False Creek.

With my eyes shut, I let my body go limp and sway with the stops, starts, and turns. I imagine I'm with the jumper's body in the water, being jostled by the currents. When I open my eyes, the cruiser is already on my street in Kitsilano. Towering trees arch over the road, shading it from the sun.

"Nice place," the cop says as she pulls up to my house. A large two-story that's had a facelift since we moved in— new dark blue siding, bright white trim.

"Thanks for the ride." I undo my seatbelt.

"I left voicemails with both your parents. I'll wait with you until one of them comes home."

"My mom's a doctor. She'll be home soon." I'm lying. I never know when she'll be home. I don't want the cop to stay—I just want to be alone. I feel like crap.

"You need to be with an adult right now."

"Look, I'm almost eighteen."

"You told me you were sixteen," she says, obviously not impressed.

"If my parents aren't home in an hour, I'll call you. I promise."

She's not biting. But then a scratchy Code 3 ... *all units ... car matching description ... south on Granville ...* call comes on her pager.

"Sounds like you're going to have to scram," I say.

"No, not leaving you." Her cellphone rings. "Constable Leong ... Yes, Dr. Winters, I'm here with your daughter ... As I explained in my message, Claire is not in any trouble ..."

I can only imagine what went through my mother's mind, hearing a voicemail from a cop.

Leong looks over at me. "She seems okay ... Yes, I'll be here with her ... see you shortly." Call ends. "Your mom will be home in about fifteen minutes."

"I've got to pee," I say.

"Let's go inside, then."

Not what I had in mind. I really want the house to myself.

I grab my backpack and helmet and open the cruiser door. Pull my bike out of the open trunk, and wheel it to the side of the house. I don't have the energy to lock it in the backyard shed. My head feels like it's floating above my body as the cop follows me up the front steps. The house looks dreamy and unfamiliar. The large front porch. Terracotta tubs bursting with red and yellow flowers. A pottery coffee mug forgotten on the small table. I stick my key into the lock, wondering if it will actually open, and it does. We enter and the door bangs shut, a loud echo ricochets off the walls. I follow the cop's gaze as she looks around: the shiny wood floors, the black leather chairs circling the fireplace in the living room, the Turkish carpets the color of blood in the dining room.

"I'm going upstairs," I say to her. "Could you just tell my mom I'll talk to her later?"

"How are you feeling?"

"Like my bladder is going to explode if I don't get to a bathroom pronto."

"You've had a shock. There's a program through victim services. I'll leave the information with your mom."

"I'm not the victim here."

She sighs. "You have my number. Be sure to call me if you remember anything else, or if you just want to talk."

As I head up the stairs, I wave at her without turning around.

After I pee, I open my bedroom door. Ribbons of late day sun the color of apricots stream in the window. I break out into another sweat as I teleport back to the Lions Gate Bridge. The jumper's face pushes its way into my mind. He stared into my eyes. Said he was sorry. Turned. Climbed over the railing. And then he was gone. Police cars. Fire trucks. Ambulances. Chaos. It couldn't have happened. I'm dreaming all this. I grab the doorframe. Squeeze the hard wood. Steady myself.

Chapter 3

I half-expect the cop to knock on my door but, thankfully, she stays downstairs. I open iTunes on my laptop, find the song of a new local hip hop band, and crank it. But the synthesized pulses and beatboxing aren't doing a thing for me. My brain is still riffing. I shut off the music. Silence, except for all the noise in my brain.

Graphic novels, Sci-Fi, books of poetry, and the odd tacky romance novel are piled on my bedside table, as well as spilling out of the bookshelf. I dig through the pile and pull out a book by Emily Dickinson. I let the book fall open to a random poem, like I always do. It opens to one I've read about a hundred times: "Hope Is the Thing with Feathers."

Hope is the thing with feathers—

That perches in the soul—

And sings the tune without the words—

And never stops—at all—

I flop onto my soft feathery duvet and read this first verse over and over. Hope. Obviously, not everyone has it perched in their souls. Did the jumper lose hope because of all the crap happening in the world and decide he could no longer live on this Earth? If so, I can totally relate. I close the book, breathe deeply, put my hand on my chest, and wait for thirty speeding heartbeats.

My cellphone bloops. Seven text messages. I can't face texting or talking to anyone right now. Not even Ty. Instead, I Google "how to find hope," and discover how in five easy steps:

1) Dream big. I dream humans will find a way to reverse climate change. Now. Right now. This very minute.

2) Accept that no one has control over their lives. Is this saying the jumper didn't have control when he climbed over the railing and hurled himself into the Burrard Inlet? Really?

3) Discontent and disorder are signs of energy and hope, not despair. If that's true, I've got hope to burn.

4) Find the benefit in whatever happens. Well, one benefit is there's one less human on the Earth using up the dwindling resources.

5) Always wonder with intense curiosity what's around the corner. An understatement.

Painting—one of the only things in my life that gives me hope in a sometimes hopeless world. I can despair and obsess endlessly about climate change, endangered species, and starvation in poor countries. But when I'm painting, everything falls away around me and I lose all track of time. With every brush stroke, a warm sensation spreads throughout my body, right to my fingers and toes. I gaze at three canvases I've painted, hanging on the wall. One of the paintings is of windswept trees lining a long road that fades into a dark gray and yellow horizon. But an ominous cloud of toxic gas hangs in the air, threatening to swallow the pastoral setting. The second painting is Earth from space, with aquamarine oceans and the outline of North and South America. Orange, yellow, and red flames lick the globe, threatening to incinerate it. The last is a self-portrait. My face is mostly in shadows with only one eye, one cheek, and my forehead clearly visible. I take this painting off the wall, slump to the floor, wrap my arms around the canvas, and hold it close.

Soft knock at the door.

"Claire," my mom says. "May I come in?" Another knock.

I get up, rehang my picture, and open the door. Mom steps into my room. The sweet spicy scent of her perfume surrounds me. Her forehead is crinkled with worry. I can't help but be amazed at how every strand of her cinnamon-colored hair is perfectly in place, even at the end of the day.

"Oh, darlin'," she says, wrapping her arms around me. "I'm so sorry you had to experience that."

My hands tentatively rest on the back of her silky, cherry-colored blazer. Sorry for me? What about the jumper? My whole body feels prickly, so I quickly disengage.

"I really want to be alone right now, Mom."

I can tell she's conflicted. "Is there anything I can get you? A cup of tea? I could make you some soup. I've got a nice butternut squash."

"Nope, but thanks anyway."

She nods. "I'll check on you later." She leaves and I close the door tightly behind her.

I'm startled by something buzzing in my backpack. I turn it upside down over my bed and shake out my wallet, a package of gum, lip gloss, hairbrush, and a book of poetry, *I Just Hope It's Lethal.* Along with sand from the beach, the jumper's cellphone lands on my bed. The ringer is obviously on vibrate. Someone is calling him. I spring back as if the phone is a grenade with the pin pulled. How did it get in my backpack? Did I put it there? It feels as if someone rammed a steel pole from my head to my guts.

Oh, my God. Oh, my God ... I have a dead guy's phone.

What do I do? Turn it in? But what if the cops ... what if ... oh, no. I'm in so much trouble ... *Don't ring again. Do not ring!* Goosebumps spread over my whole body like a bad rash.

The phone feels heavy in my hand. The lock screen has a photo of the jumper chugging a large mug of beer. Missed call from Jarret. Written on a tiny piece of paper taped to the back of the phone are the numbers 4564. Either he had a seriously bad memory, or he wanted someone to check out his phone. Searching a stranger's phone is kind of like reading their diary. Not cool. I circle my thumb around the home button for a long time before I press it. I toss the cellphone on my bed, stare at it.

But I can't help myself. I grab it and press the home button for another look at the jumper. Enter the passcode. I could get into serious trouble for keeping the phone. It might have important contacts, photographs, fingerprints ...

I lie on my bed with the phone in my hand. My mind spins out of control. Maybe the guy was a member of the Red Scorpions gang and skimmed money from a lucrative drug deal or prostitution ring he was in charge of. Instead of facing the inevitable, getting decapitated by the gang boss and his goons—cement blocks tied to his feet and thrown into the harbor, or blown to smithereens with a submachine gun—he took matters into his own hands. He actually looked more like a bike courier who intercepted an important document from a major financial empire, implicating the bigwigs of fraud, and he somehow got caught up in the white-collar espionage, and he was going to blow the whistle and everyone knew he knew, and he figured his days were numbered because the bigwigs had connections to a notorious hitman.

But what if it was worse than that? What if he was just an ordinary guy who couldn't find a good enough reason to live?

Chapter 4

I wake up to blinding sunlight and the snap-snap-snap as my window shade rolls up. My sister's face is about an inch from mine. She looks like she's wearing those fake glasses with weird painted-on eyes.

"Geez, Belle, I'm trying to sleep."

I'm covered in a blanket. Still have my clothes on. I pull out the one earbud still stuck in my ear and look at the clock. I've slept for almost eighteen hours. My brain's foggy. Did I dream all this up? The Lions Gate? The jumper? But it isn't a dream. I remember the jumper walking, laughing, holding onto the railing.

"T-t-time to get up, Claire. G-g-get up."

"It's my day off. Get out of my room and just let me

sleep." I roll over and cover my head with the pillow.

"Guess what, C-Claire? Last night we watched a movie. And Daddy made p-p-popcorn. He did."

Belle was born nineteen years ago with Down syndrome. Her almond-shaped eyes are spaced too far apart and her tiny ears look crinkled. Despite my mother's best efforts at signing her up for every activity for "special" people—such as skating, volleyball, swimming, gymnastics, jazzercise, and belly dancing—Belle is still a chub. A serious chub. She has enormous boobs and an ass that spills over most chairs. There's nothing subtle about my sister. She barrels around like a truck with psychedelic flashing lights, horn honking, and quadraphonic stereo blasting. Belle's ridiculously happy most of the time, finding joy in the weirdest things, like watching an ant carry a leaf or a stick twice its size, big, fat, snowflakes, clowns, and *Friends* reruns. In a nano-second, she can flip a crazy switch and win an Oscar for "Best Conniption Fit," the way she throws herself down on the floor, yowling in anguish. But in a matter of minutes, she's distracted by a speck of dirt or a thread on the carpet where her head is resting. Or, she'll see a tiny spider and hold it in her hand, and want to make it a proper home and find friends for it.

"You're supposed to g-get up, Claire."

"Says who?"

"Me says. It's lunchtime already. Daddy says he'll make us pancakes, with blueberries. You hungry? You hungry, Claire?"

"No, I'm not hungry!" I pull the covers over my head.

She yanks them right off and lets out a wheezy laugh that sounds like she's chain-smoked for thirty years. She lies down beside me and cuddles up. I'm not going to win this battle, so I wrap my arm around her.

"What'd you dream last night, Belle?"

"Dunno."

"Yes, you do."

"No, I don't."

"You always remember your dreams."

She thinks for a moment. "Oh, yeah. N-n-now I remember. I do. A teeny, tiny bird was in my hand, right here." She holds out her hand and circles her palm with a finger.

"What did it look like?"

"It was pretty. So, so many colors ... like green and orange."

"What did the bird do?"

"It was dead. I pet it, and pet it and pet it and pet it."

"Then what happened?"

"It was no more dead."

"Then what?" I ask.

"Then it flew away up. R-right up to the sun," she says, and flings her arms over her head. "Way, way, way up high to the sun."

"Cool."

"Yeah, c-cool."

We cuddle a few minutes more.

"Belle, can you keep a secret?"

"Yeah, I can keep secrets. Lots and lots of secrets."

"Something happened yesterday. Something horrible."

Dad's usual rhythmic knock taps at the door.

"May we come in, Claire?" Dad says.

"What is this? A family meeting?" I call out.

The door opens a crack and Dad peeks in.

"Can't a girl sleep in on her day off?" I ask. "Geez."

"Just checking in with you," he says as Mom follows him into my room. Dad has obviously been painting in his studio, cadmium red and Hansa yellow splotched on his khaki shorts, and I can smell the paint thinner he uses to clean his brushes. And Mom is just back from one of her marathon-training runs. Her cheeks are pink with a film of sweat.

"Belle, we'd like to talk to Claire for a minute," Mom says. "How about you make your bed and put your clothes away."

Belle's shoulders droop and she lets out a drama-queen sigh. "But what about the secret?" My parents look at me curiously as Belle slumps out of my room. What possessed me to think it was a good idea to tell Belle about the jumper? She would have totally freaked. I'm an idiot.

Dad sits on the bed and gently brushes my matted hair off my face. "So?"

"So what?" I feel tired and bitchy.

"We checked in on you last night but you were fast asleep," Dad says.

I look around my room, rather than at their concerned

gazes; watch the dust motes floating in the sunlight that streams through the window.

"Did you know him?" Mom says. "Tell us what happened, sweetie."

"Kathryn." Dad gives her the "chill out" look. "Let's let Claire have some space. We can talk when she's up for it."

"But this is serious, Phillip."

"Dad's right. I need some space to process everything."

They don't move. Just stare at me.

"It's not as if I knew the guy or anything," I tell them.

"You didn't know him?" Mom says.

I shrug.

"Still, it must have been a shock," Mom says.

Dad stands. "You know your mother and I are here for you."

"Got it." I would like to argue that this isn't always the case, but what's the point?

They linger, hoping I'll change my mind and spill my guts. Dad inspects my paintings hanging on the wall. I can see the artist's gears spinning in his head. Mom cleans out dirt from under her right thumbnail with her left pointer fingernail. She spreads all her fingers out and checks the others, crosses her arms again, and looks at me.

The jumper's cellphone rings. Under the blanket. I must have had it in my hand when I fell asleep. They look at where the ringing is coming from, then look at me.

"You changed your ring tone?" Mom says.

"Yup."

Both take one long last look at me, leave the room, and close the door quietly behind them.

Call display shows a 1-888 number. Must be a telemarketer.

I feel so alone. How can I talk to anybody about seeing a guy jump off a bridge? Who would truly understand what I'm feeling?

I rummage in the drawer beside my bed and take out a new blank journal and the calligraphy pen my aunt bought me for my birthday. The tan cover with a white box on the front reads: *Live the Life You Imagine*. The binding cracks when I open it. I stick my face into the blank pages; they smell like vanilla. I was going to use it for a sketchbook but I have a better idea.

Hi, it's me. Claire. The last person on Earth to see you alive before you took a dive off the Lions Gate Bridge. The last person to hear you speak. I'm sorry. Your last words. Why were you sorry? For messing up the lives of those who love you? Or were you sorry for me? Did you know that after watching you jump to your death, I'd feel like a two-ton block of cement is crushing me? I keep playing it over and over in my head, and I wonder if there was something I could have done to change your mind. If I'd reacted quicker. If I hadn't stood there like a zombie, not quite believing what I was seeing.

I sometimes think of offing myself. The reckless things human beings are doing to destroy this planet are more than I can bear sometimes: burning the Amazon jungles to make room for cattle, sending toxic waste to poor countries, sucking every last drop

of fossil fuels out of the ground while our
planet roasts. My parents get worried
about my dark moods that sometimes
last too long. But it's not me that has the
problem, it's the messed-up world I live in.

If I can figure out why you ended your
life, maybe in some weird way it will help
me find a good reason to keep living mine.
Or, who knows? Maybe you'll convince me
to join you.

I flop back onto my pillow. The scene on the bridge loops nonstop in slow motion. The guy looking down into the water. Turning to me with those navy blue eyes. Handing me his phone. Saying he's sorry. Heaving himself up on the railing. Jumping. White shirt puffing up. Disappearing out of sight. Splash! I didn't actually hear the splash, but I add that for effect.

And ... repeat.

I imagine I'm in a movie, and the director wants to shoot a different ending.

An-n-n-nd Action!

Soundtrack starts low, the tone ominous, like you know something terrifying is about to happen any second. The volume increases.

Medium Shot: Claire, age sixteen, cool but not too cool, artsy, fairly bright, doesn't break any mirrors, bikes across the Lions Gate Bridge on the southeast sidewalk. The music pounds out as cars whizz by in both directions, foreshadowing the frenetic energy to come.

Extremely Wide Shot of the western sky shows the July sun is low and orangey on the horizon, casting an eerie glow on the sailboats, ships, and tugboats on the Burrard Inlet.

Medium Close-Up: Claire gets off her bike, takes out her phone to snap some photos. She spots a hot guy in his twenties. (Scrap that.) Claire spots a very hot guy in his twenties walking toward her, talking on a cellphone. Claire zooms in on him with the camera in her phone and snaps a pic.

Over-the-Shoulder: Hot guy laughs and ends his call. Claire takes another photo. She walks closer to him. The music volume softens.

Medium Close-Up: He stops. Looks over the railing, stares into the water. Claire takes two more photos.

Extreme Close Up: He looks at Claire with those amazing eyes that remind her of denim.

Camera pulls back. "I'm sorry," he says. He hands Claire his cellphone and starts to climb onto the railing.

Camera pulls back to *Wide Shot.* The soundtrack rises to an aching crescendo.

"Don't jump," Claire screams.

Soundtrack is loud, frenetic guitar riffs, drums pounding.

Claire, who has freakishly quick reflexes, grabs his arm and pulls him back onto the walkway.

He hauls himself back up on the railing with one leg over. More guitar and heavy drumming.

Medium Shot: Once again, Claire strong-arms him back down. Music volume softens.

Close Up on the guy, sitting on the walkway, head in his hands.

Close Up on Claire, looking frantic as she talks on her cellphone.

The camera pulls back to show Claire with her comforting hand on the guy's shoulder. His arm covers his face while his body shakes with sobs.

Drone Shot while a mournful soundtrack plays softly in the background. The camera rises higher and higher as a last funnel of sun shines on the bridge before it sinks behind the mountains. In the dusky light, the flashing red lights of two police cruisers and an ambulance pull up to them.

Cut!

Then reality bleeds in, and the guy's over the railing before I know it.

Chapter 5

At the front door, Mom and Dad wait while I help Belle wriggle into her sweater.

"We'll miss you," Mom says, obviously disappointed.

"Something's come up, that's all," I say. Mom looks at me all doctorly, trying to figure out if they should be leaving me on my own.

"How can you m-m-miss 'Dinosaurs Alive,' Claire? It's at the Science Centre."

"I know where the exhibit is, Belle," I snap and then immediately regret it.

"And we're going out for dinner after." Belle shakes with excitement. "I'm having n-n-nachos. With guacamole and salsa."

"Wish you could've joined us," Dad says, reaching for the door handle. He's clearly disappointed, too. "Another time."

"Our family time is so precious," Mom says. I try not to let her hurt look stab at my heart.

"Y-yeah, Claire. Family time is precious," Belle echoes.

What I really want to say is our time together wouldn't be so *precious* if both my parents would chill out with their workaholic lives. And that maybe they could spend a bit more time with me—just me—rather than focusing all their attention on Belle.

"Sorry. Next time ... I promise," I say, trying to sound like I mean it.

Belle stomps her feet and sticks out her bottom lip in an exaggerated pout. Dad opens the door and they file out.

I pedal my bike as fast as I can, dodging potholes, trying to keep up with the traffic heading east on Broadway. Beeps and honks drown out purring car engines. Exhaust from a UPS truck burns my throat as it chugs by. Right in front of me, a rusted-out Mazda is cut off by a gold SUV, fresh from the car wash, sloughing off beads of water. The Mazda screeches to a stop. My front tire crushes against the back bumper. I fly over my handlebars and hit the back of the car. When I roll onto the ground, my helmet bounces as it smacks against the pavement.

As he gets out of his car, Mazda guy yells, "Fucking asshole!" at the suv and flips the finger. Traffic lines up behind me.

"You hurt?" says Mazda guy, his white muscle shirt showing off totem-pole tattoos down both his arms.

"I don't think so." I slowly stand up and brush dust and dirt off my shorts. I feel shaky.

He lifts my bike upright and guides me by the elbow to the sidewalk. "Bike didn't get damaged." He looks down at my scraped knee. "Want me to drive you somewhere?"

"No. But thanks."

"Didn't even get that moron's license plate number," he growls, then gets back into his car and drives off, easing the traffic jam.

I stay on the sidewalk and weave my bike through a stream of people hobbling with bulging shopping bags or waiting for buses.

The concrete-block police station has a band of shiny rust-brown marble at street level, with *Vancouver Police* in tall white letters. I lock my bike to a green lamppost. In my jean jacket pocket, my fingertips rub the smooth screen of the jumper's cellphone. Constable Leong will probably ask why I didn't tell her about the cellphone in the first place. Will she believe me, that in my head-mush, I totally forgot the jumper gave it to me? Totally forgot I put it in my backpack. Totally forgot to tell her I touched his white shirt with my fingertips before he went over the railing. My gut knots up. I'll quickly hand over the cellphone and leave. A drop and dash.

I trudge up the steps to the glass doors, peer in, and see uniformed officers crisscrossing the foyer. What if they want to question me again? Could I be charged with theft? Or worse? A breeze skims over me. It feels cold in my armpits, where I'm sweating like crazy.

I pull open the heavy door. Cool air whooshes from inside. I feel like a criminal turning myself in. One wall is covered with photos. Not of bank robbers, like I'd imagined, but of missing people. If the guy had jumped off the Lions

Gate late at night, with no one around to witness it, his face could have been on this wall, too. One girl, Angela Jardine, has been missing since November 9, 2018. Aged fifteen, 5'4", 112 pounds, she looks a bit like me—light green eyes and golden hair just past her shoulders. She doesn't wear makeup, either. But her nose is a bit crooked, and her cheeks look like they were rubbed raw with sandpaper.

"Can I help you?" A beefy male officer towers over me. His moustache looks like an enormous brown caterpillar.

The jumper's cellphone rings in my pocket. "Need to take that?" he asks.

"Yeah, I'd better."

"Check in at reception when you're ready." He turns and flags down another uniform and disappears behind a door.

I grab the cellphone out of my jacket. Call display says *Danielle*. Cops hover all around while I hack into the jumper's voicemail. My hand shakes. That annoying woman's voice: *Who's calling please? Enter your access code and then press pound.* I punch in the same code 4-5-6-4 #. It doesn't work. *Are you sure you have the right access code?* I try about ten different variations of the numbers. *I can't accept that code.* Finally, I type the numbers backwards: 4-6-5-4. It works. *You have one unheard message and four saved messages.*

"Hi, it's me. I've been waiting for you. Did you forget again?" Her voice sounds soft and patient. Big sigh. "Well ... I guess if I don't hear from you, I'll just cab it home ... What's going on with you? The way you've been acting lately is starting to freak me right out." Long pause. "You know I love you, right? Call me and let me know how you're doing. I don't care how late it is."

I feel sick that Danielle—probably the jumper's girl-friend—doesn't even know what happened to him. Will the cops care why this guy offed himself? Will they investigate the case in detail, like on CSI, until his family and friends have all the answers they need to go on with their lives? Or are the cops only interested in getting him to the morgue so they can hunt down murderers and heroin dealers?

My knee stings as I walk to the reception counter holding the cellphone.

"What can I do for you?" The officer behind the counter scratches a long white scar on his shiny forehead.

"Is Constable Leong around?"

"She's away from the station right now. Probably won't be back for a few hours."

The front door swings open. A woman cop holds the elbow of a handcuffed guy about my age, wearing torn stonewashed jeans and a black T-shirt with *Cannibal Corpse* in dripping bloody letters, and guides him across the foyer.

"Like I keep telling you, you got nuthin' on me," the guy says, hiding behind his shaggy brown hair.

"And like I keep telling you—withholding evidence, obstructing justice—and that's just for starters," says the cop in a firm but quiet voice.

She leads him through a door. Probably heading for a jail cell. Is that where I'll end up when they find out I kept the jumper's cellphone? I've got to get out of here.

"Want to leave a message for Constable Leong?" the cop asks me.

"Thanks, but I'll just call her later."

I slip the cellphone back into my jacket, turn around, and bolt for the exit. I press my body into the glass door that opens to the rush of people and traffic.

As I bike home, black clouds race to cover the summer sky and the air smells like rain. The jumper's cellphone in my pocket feels heavy as a boulder.

After I lock my bike in the backyard shed, I stop outside Dad's studio and look in the dark windows. Usually it would be a no-brainer. Whenever I have an evening to myself, I paint in the studio for hours until I can't keep my eyes open any longer. But I can't face it tonight. My brain is a jumbled mess.

I unlock the back door to the kitchen. A bowl of peaches sits on the shiny island. With my brain on overload, I'm happy to have the house all to myself. The only sound is the chugging of the fridge. I rummage in the freezer, pull out a bag of frozen beans, and head for the TV room.

I plop myself down into one of the most comfortable chairs in the house, soft velvety fabric that swallows me up. With all the chatter going on in my head, watching TV is the last thing I feel like doing. As soon as I crunch on my first frozen bean, there's a text on the jumper's phone.

It's from Danielle: *Where are you? Please call me. I'm worried sick!!*

Geez. It's been over twenty-four hours since he jumped and she still doesn't know? I really want to call her and tell her what happened. But I can't. I'm such a chicken. Besides, then the word would get out that I have his cellphone. How else would I know her number? Instead, I scroll through the other texts. Most read like a conversation between cavemen.

From Dave:

Whassup bitch?

Nada

A jug at Malones?

Beauty

From Steve:

I'm broke buy me some weed

No

Come on, you always have cash

Still no

Later A-hole

I scroll through several more texts, then check out the list of phone calls. Yesterday at 3:46 PM. It was Jarret he was talking to, the one who made him laugh just before he jumped. I remember the jumper's face breaking out into a big smile. Can hear his laugh.

I hack into his voicemail. The first saved voice message is from a guy named Chris: "Hey bro, we missed you at the Shark Club last night. Didn't you get my text? The game was superb, in case you missed it. So ... hope you're hanging in there. You've been M.I.A.. lately ... What's up with that? Wish I knew what was going on in that warped brain of yours. Anyway ... call me back soon."

I'm in deep now. There are three other saved voice messages.

Second saved message: "You'd better drag your sorry ass to the field tonight because we're playing Westside. I want your cleat firmly imprinted on that dickhead center's ass. Hey, did you really punch out some guy at Keefer Bar the other night? If so, epic. Wish I was there to see that. Oh yeah, and you also owe me a pint. Later."

Third saved message. "Will, it's Mom. Did you get my other messages? I've left a few. Haven't seen or heard from you in a few weeks now. Starting to get worried. Is everything all right? Call me when you get this message. Please, dear."

I recall his smile, his eyes, his wavy brown hair. The name Will suits him.

Fourth saved message: "What's wrong with you? Why aren't you returning Mom's calls? You know how much she worries about you. Don't be a jerk. Just call her."

Obviously, Will has a sister.

I swipe through too many photos of drunk-looking guys holding up pints of beer and/or flipping the finger and/or mooning the camera. Several other photos of the same guys playing soccer, muscular legs stretching for the ball, jumping for a head butt, happy faces in a group hug. A few shots from North Vancouver looking south, ships anchored in the Strait of Georgia. Photos of a girl, alone, probably Danielle from the voicemail. She looks about nineteen or twenty and could be on the cover of *Vogue*—with creamy skin, sparkling hair the color of wheat. Her small turned-up nose and large round brown eyes looked perfectly symmetrical. A face I would like to sketch. Several more selfies of the girlfriend and Will together: at Jericho Beach, outside on the patio of

Has Bean, a popular East Van coffee shop, on the seawall at Stanley Park. One shot was taken above her on the bed— arms crossed behind her head, naked from the waist up. Another photo was taken from exactly the same angle but she is laughing hilariously, her body bent over slightly.

I thumb through dozens of images so disturbing I feel dizzy. Selfies of Will standing against the same gray wall, dark and shadowy. He looks into the camera with the saddest, most desperate expressions. In a few photos, his eyes are bloodshot red. There's a bunch of photos of Will with a gun. The gun looks fake, like a plastic toy, but the photos still give me the chills. Will cradles the gun in his arms, rocking it like a baby; the barrel points directly at his heart; at his temple, with finger ready to pull the trigger; the barrel right in his mouth as he stares into the camera, eyes almost serene. I imagine cradling a real gun. Aiming it at my heart. Pointing the barrel to my temple. Pulling the trigger. Kaboom!

I eat half the bag of frozen beans, lie down on the couch, and pull the knitted blanket over me. I breathe deeply a few times, swipe the home screen, and go right to "Notes."

There's only one.

There was one thing in my life that was important to me. One thing that got me up every morning with a big fucking smile on my face. One thing that I was good at and gave me hope for my future. When that was taken away, there wasn't much left to hang around for. People are going to say I'm selfish for killing myself when I have family and friends who love me. But they don't understand. If they were in my shoes they'd probably do the same. I would have been a useless piece of shit if I just kept living my life like an empty shell. I am sorry for those I left behind, but I know they will be better off without me in the long run.

Will

What was that one important thing that was taken away from Will? So important that he ended his life over it.

Chapter 6

"Mine," Izzy yells out as she runs to the volleyball net. Her poofy pink vintage dress with a huge bow isn't exactly beach volleyball apparel. Then again, neither are my jeans and T-shirt. The summer rain chases away the Kits Beach volleyball keeners—fit girls who wear skimpy shorts and sports bras, hunky guys.

Izzy double-fists the ball over the net to Ty. "Got it!" Ty says as he leaps up and smashes it over the net.

Declan makes a spectacular dive into the sand and somehow manages to get the ball into the air. He jumps back on his feet. "Take that!" He gets his black hair and dark brown skin and eyes from his Indo-Canadian mom, and his weird name from his Irish dad. I met the three of them last fall when I joined Earth Rescue, a local environmental group for teens. The group is involved with activities like removing invasive species and planting native ones in city parks, weeding community gardens, and writing letters to Vancouver City Council to lobby for a plastic-bag-free city.

Soon after I got to know them, Ty's mom Tessa hired Izzy and me to work at the Cosmic Cow (a.k.a. the cc), the café she owns.

Izzy slaps the ball and it dribbles over the net right in front of me. My brain and body refuse to coordinate; the ball falls between my hands, hits me on the head, and lands in the sand. Everybody groans.

"Sorry," I say. "I'm such a klutz today."

"No kidding." Ty playfully tackles me to the ground. The damp sand feels hard when I fall on my back and my scraped knee stings a little. Ty has a silly grin as he sits on me, straddling my waist, holding me down by the wrists. He leans down, kisses me gently. I wriggle out of his grasp and climb on top of him. I brush sand out of his mop of Hawaiian-surfer blond curls and the white whiskers sprouting on his cheeks and pointy chin.

"Get a room, you two," Izzy says as she wipes sand off her feet. Declan already has his sneakers on.

Ty and I stand, brush off the remaining sand. He stuffs the volleyball into his backpack. I dig into my purse and hand each of them compostable bags to collect garbage on the beach. Items like potato chip bags, empty juice boxes, and plastic bottles that people just throw on the ground, too damn lazy or careless to deal with them. In his backpack, Ty also carries a super-thick work glove and a box for the used drug needles we sometimes find. Cleaning up natural spaces is our regular routine whenever we go to a park or a beach.

Izzy picks up an empty beer can, and then skips off to catch a candy bar wrapper that's being carried by a breeze. Declan pushes off on his skateboard, stopping to pick up garbage along the paved walkway.

My brain is still in a gloomy fog and everything feels surreal. I bend over to pick up a plastic cup and feel faint. I stand and look around to calm my wooziness. The rays of sun peeking through the clouds light up raindrops still clinging to leaves, like tiny Christmas lights. Willow trees with trunks like giant elephant legs line the paths.

The North Shore Mountains poke up through the clouds across the inlet. The Burrard Inlet. The body of water Will jumped into. A shiver zaps through my body.

"Cold?" Ty asks. "I've got a sweatshirt if you want." I shake my head and hold the garbage bag with both hands to stop it from trembling.

"You seem a bit spacey today. Something going on?" Ty says, picking up an empty takeout coffee cup.

"Nope." I veer off in a different direction, feeling like my head might float right off my body.

After we've combed most of the beach, we empty our bags into the proper bins by the concession stand. I've hardly picked up anything. Out of his bag, Ty picks out a thick, rectangular piece of plastic with four screws on each corner. He inspects it closely, plops it into his backpack instead of the garbage.

"Claire, you gotta see *Waking Life*," Izzy says, dropping a few empty cans into the large recycling bin.

"The art is pretty innovative," Declan says, opening the lid to the garbage bin and dumping in the contents of his bag.

"Yeah, it was shot in video and then computer-generated to look like animation," Ty says, emptying his garbage bag.

"It's called rotoscoping," Declan says, not in a know-it-all kind of way. He just seems to understand these things.

"Did they use some kind of digital equipment?" Ty says.

"Not exactly sure. I think it's more of an animation technique—tracing over film footage, frame by frame," Declan says.

"We've got to try it," Ty says. "I'll hunt for some sixteen millimeter film and an old projector at the junk store."

After all our bags are empty, Izzy doles out hand sanitizer. My skin stings as I rub my hands together.

We head down the path toward the Planetarium. Declan skateboards slowly beside us. All I see from the side is the tip of his nose under his hoodie.

"What was the film about?" I ask.

"The main guy was totally, like, in a weird lucid dream where he visits all these people who talk about enlightenment and philosophy and stuff," Izzy says, retying the brilliant pink ribbon on her dress.

"Sounds cool," I say. I feel like I'm living a weird lucid dream. "What kind of philosophy?" I ask Declan, one of the smartest people I know. He and I sometimes share books and talk about them. He has a mind that examines everything he reads and comes up with ideas, interpretations, and conclusions that go right over my head. I feel smarter just being around him. But I wonder if he sometimes gets bored with us.

Declan pulls off his hoodie. "The movie kind of threw everything out there—Buddhism, Taoism, existentialism ... A bit too much, actually."

"A mind bender," Ty says.

"Basically, the film is asking what's more real—dreams or waking life?" Declan says. "And how are we supposed to 'wake up' to the true nature of reality?"

"And where do we fit in, in the grand scheme of things?" Ty says.

"I like where the movie talked about time being an illusion," Izzy says. "And the only thing that's real is right this moment. And this one."

"And this one, and this one," Ty says. Izzy giggles.

Away down the path, an old man with Einstein hair sits on a bench, looking out at the ocean. Izzy runs ahead of us and sits down beside him. He looks at her like he can't quite believe she's real. Her spiky white-blonde hair and dramatic turquoise eye shadow make her look like a living cartoon. Izzy's goal in life is to make as many old people smile as she can. As she talks to him, her hands wave all over the place. Her laugh sounds like a hyena. When we arrive at the bench, the man is definitely smiling. Mission accomplished.

"Hey, guys," Izzy says to us. "Come and meet Arthur."

"Hello," says Arthur.

We all say "hi" and stand around awkwardly.

"Well, you have an awesome day, Arthur," Izzy says and stands up. "And don't forget to tell your wife the joke."

"Will do," says Arthur, shaking his head, not really sure what just hit him.

We head toward the Planetarium. "Do you really have to chat with every stranger who crosses your path, Izzy?" Declan says.

"Depression is a big problem with the elderly in this

country. Men in their eighties have a higher risk of suicide than any other age group. Even teenagers," Izzy says.

"Really? More than teenagers?" Ty says.

"It's true—I saw it on a show called *Health Watch*."

"Speaking of suicide," Declan says, "I read on my news feed that somebody jumped off the Lions Gate the other day."

A tidal wave builds in my body.

"Did he live?" Izzy asks.

"What do you think, genius?" Ty says.

"He could have landed on a raft or a cruise ship or something," Izzy says.

"Yeah, like there are so many rafts floating in the harbor just waiting to catch jumpers," Ty says. He sometimes gets impatient with Izzy's crazy notions.

"People have survived jumps before," she responds, "even off bridges that are way bigger than the Lions Gate. I saw this show once where cameras were set up on the Golden Gate Bridge in San Francisco every day for a year. Twenty-four jumpers tried to commit suicide and some of them actually lived."

"If I was going to off myself, I sure as hell wouldn't

dive off a bridge," Ty says and turns to Declan. "Gas, gun, or rope?"

Declan thinks for a moment. "Definitely gas. Less messy."

"I'd OD," says Izzy. "Much more romantic."

"What would you OD on? Cinnamon hearts?" Ty says. The guys have a good laugh.

The blood slowly drains from my head. "I was there." I choke out the words. My head feels even fuzzier and my gut knots up.

"Where?" Ty says.

"On the bridge. The Lions Gate." My hands won't stop shaking. "I saw the guy jump." Everyone stops moving, as if they'd stepped in cement, and stare at me with big eyes.

"Oh, my God!" Izzy says, covering her mouth with her hand. "You actually saw the guy jump?"

"You're joking, right?" says Declan.

I shake my head and feel like puking.

"What were you doing on the bridge?" Ty asks.

It feels like I have rocks in my mouth when I talk. "I was going to North Van ... stopped on the bridge. Took some photos. He jumped right in front of me."

"Are you serious?" says Ty.

"Did you talk to him?" Declan asks.

I shake my head. If they knew he'd spoken to me, they'd wonder why I didn't talk him out of jumping. A guilty panic shoots through me.

"Did you see the body? Did it sink in the water?" Izzy asks.

I shrug.

Everyone just stands there. Declan looks up at the trees. Ty's glance darts around as if he's watching a ping pong match. Then Izzy wraps her bamboo-thin arms around me in a long warm hug. Unlike the Grinch, Izzy's heart is two sizes too big. I thought telling my friends would feel like a crane lifting the huge boulder off my chest. Instead, the weight feels even heavier. We walk quietly for a bit. Ty grabs hold of my hand. Squeezes it gently. Izzy runs across the street and uproots a few flowers from someone's front yard and runs back. Not exactly a "good neighbor" thing to do.

"We need to pay our respects to the jumper," she says.

"His name is Will," I say, almost too quiet to hear.

"How do you know his name?" Ty asks.

I ignore the question. Don't want to get busted.

"Will. Nice, like Prince William." Izzy smiles. "Stand around me." The wind blows Izzy's long peacock-feather earrings.

Like idiots, we stand in a circle. Ty is so close to me, I can feel the warmth of his body.

"Now look up. To Will's soul, wherever it may be." Izzy throws the stolen bouquet as high as she can. Soggy flowers rain down on us. A few petals land in my mouth but I don't mind.

The hot sun has finally burned off the clouds and dried up last night's rain. We walk toward Vanier Park, sit on the grass, and watch the kayakers and sailboat traffic in English Bay. I get a glimpse of the Burrard Bridge. Even though it's not the Lions Gate, it's still a bridge, and something rumbles deep inside of me. I start to sweat. Flashbacks puncture my mind. Will's eyes. A breeze tousling his wavy brown hair. His fingers gripped on the railing. I change position and sit where the bridge is out of my sight. I'm so deep inside my head, it feels like I'm wearing a burqa, like some Muslim women wear, and I can only see out of the tiny woven squares. The three of them talk and talk but it buzzes in my brain, like when a radio station isn't quite tuned in.

When the sun sinks low in the sky, Izzy and Declan get up to leave. "You pushin' caffeine tomorrow?" Izzy asks me.

I nod. It's hard to even imagine tomorrow.

"*Au revoir, mon amie*. Take care of yourself. Have a bubble bath or something," she says and kisses me gently on the cheek. "Call me if you need to talk. Anytime. Even three or four in the morning. You know I'm always here for you."

"Ditto, Claire," Declan says. "Reach out if you need to." Izzy stands on his skateboard and he pushes her down the path. She squeals when he tries to go too fast.

"You're shaking," Ty says, tightly wrapping his arm around my shoulder. We walk to where his '79 Volkswagen van is parked. We both climb in.

"Where do you want to go?" he says, pushing the key into the ignition.

"Anywhere. Just drive." The van engine chugs a few times before it starts. I stretch out my legs, my feet on the dash, and open the window. My hair tickles my face like a thousand feathers as we drive.

With the help of manuals and YouTube videos, Ty single-handedly rebuilt the van engine, piece by piece, scrounging parts at scrapyards or ordering them on eBay. His mechanical genius is what I first found attractive about him. Well, maybe after his wide-open smile, broad shoulders, and goofy sense of humor. And I love that he's trying to save the planet by reusing and recycling stuff that other people would throw into the landfill.

Ty can build, fix, or upcycle almost anything. Tessa, his mom, says that he must have gotten his mechanical abilities from his father, who buggered off when Ty was still in the womb. Ty's inventions include: a toaster out of an old VHS player, a Wi-Fi radio out of a small suitcase—and for my birthday last year, he gave me a bike light he made me out of a deodorant stick. Not the most romantic gift, but it sure is practical. He doesn't have a "real" summer job, but he makes good money fixing broken stuff: toaster ovens, bicycles, clock radios, stereos, washing machines, lawn mowers. He sells them on eBay or Craigslist.

He got Declan, Izzy, and me to help him paint the van like a 60s hippie magic bus with rainbows, peace signs, and flowers. A perfect vehicle to park outside of Tessa's retro Cosmic Cow Café.

Sometimes, Ty and I drive around honking and waving at total strangers and then laugh our asses off. Or we drive to Mountain View Cemetery, lie down in the grassy area between the tombstones, and look for dragons in the clouds. It can only be dragons, not elephants or aliens or castles. When we spot one, we have to make up a story, but not about dragons. I usually start the story and then we tag-team to the end.

I don't feel like storytelling or laughing at strangers today. After driving around the university, we end up at Spanish Banks. Ty goes to the back of the van and opens the dusty burlap curtains to let in some light. The van isn't exactly equipped for camping. It doesn't have cupboards, a fridge, or a stove. It's empty except for toolboxes and a wooden bench that folds down into a bed. He installed two frayed seat belts for the bench for when Declan and Izzy join us. If there's ever a fifth person, someone has to sit in a lawn chair that usually tips over whenever Ty turns a corner.

He straightens out a wool blanket on top of the thick foamie that looks like a bear took big bites out of it. "Come here."

I go to the back of the van and lie down on my back beside him. He smells like a wet dog rolled in onions, which surprisingly doesn't bother me too much. He leans over, kisses me gently on the lips, then lies back down.

"What do you think happens after you die?" I ask.

"You become worm food."

"Serious."

"No idea."

"Come on. You've got to have a theory."

Ty sticks his finger in a hole in the blanket. "I'm counting on being around for a while, so I've never really thought about it much."

"I didn't either until ..."

Ty rolls on his side and props up his head with his hand. "Here's my theory. When we die, our spirits leave our bodies and kind of float to another galaxy, either to some planet or a moon, or maybe even into a black hole."

"Why another galaxy?"

"For intergalactic breeding. Anyways, there's a roll-call and kind of an interview."

"Who's interviewing?"

"Some big cheese. He asks you some questions—"

"Why can't it be a 'she' big cheese?"

"All right, based on how you answer *her* questions, your spirit zooms through kind of a vortex to another planet where you morph into some life form, have sex, make alien babies, and—"

"And live happily ever after," I say.

"Something like that."

He gives me one of those kisses that usually shoots through my body, sending a powerful tingling right down to my toes. But I feel numb. I wrap one of his long blond curls around my finger and look into his eyes, the color of chocolate drops.

"That bridge thing really messed with you, didn't it?" Ty asks.

I nod.

"Can't even imagine." He turns onto his back, hands behind his head.

I really want him to just hold me, stroke my head, kiss my forehead, and tell me I'm going to feel better. But I'm too afraid to ask.

Chapter 7

"Hey," Ty cups my cheek with his hand. "Anything I can do?" We lean against his van outside my house.

I shake my head. "I'll be fine." My new mantra. *I'm fine ... I'm fine ... I'm fine ...* Why can't I tell him how I really feel? That it's like I'm a passenger in my own body. Just floating high above, and everything around me looking phony and far away. Why am I so afraid to tell anyone? Except a dead guy, that is.

"I'll probably drop by the cc tomorrow," he says.

"Guess I'll see you, then."

We kiss and he wraps me in a big hug, lifts me off the ground, and spins me. But it's as if a dentist missed with his needle and froze my whole body instead of just my mouth.

I wheel my bike to the backyard where Belle and Dad are in the middle of their bizarre evening ritual. This is how it goes: Mom asks Belle to fetch Dad for dinner. Belle stands outside the studio window and taps. Dad first hides, then jumps in front of the window and scares the heck out of her. This makes her holler and screech like someone being chased with a chainsaw. They repeat this over and over and over and over, until Dad's finally had it or he's hungry enough to come in. Belle never has enough. I sometimes feel jealous of the fun they have together. My father is fairly stoic, but his face lights up with the biggest smile when he and Belle go through their routine. Even if I did handstands and backflips, I doubt Dad would notice.

Belle runs over and tries to hug me.

"Not now, Belle. I have to put my bike in the shed." All of a sudden I feel super cranky.

"Where were you, Claire? Did you see Ty? Were you with T-Ty?" Belle says.

"Yes, I was with Ty."

"You were kissing Ty, weren't you, Claire?"

"Get out of my face for once, Belle." Her smile disintegrates. She runs to Dad who's at the studio door. He looks over at me, disappointed.

I walk into the kitchen. The smell of onions, garlic, and fresh basil wafts through the air. As usual, Mom is whipping up another example of her culinary wizardry. She's Type A superhuman. Besides being a gourmet cook, she works as much as ten hours a day as a family doctor—sometimes more. She's a competitive marathon runner, works out at the gym, practices yoga, and also paddles with a dragon boat team. She volunteers as a board member for Vancouver Community Connections, an organization that helps people with developmental disabilities, and she sometimes volunteers at a free health clinic on the Downtown Eastside. She supports Dad's art business by going to tons of openings and showings a year. And she's involved in Belle's life and activities. She uses every waking moment of every day, doing something productive. I sometimes wish there was a little more space in her calendar for me.

"Hi," she says as she stirs vegetables in a wok. Chicken marinates on a plate close by.

"Hey."

She turns to face me, leaving the skillet on the burner. "You look so pale." She puts her doctorly hand on my forehead.

"I'm worried about you, Claire." She quickly goes back to her stir-frying. "So, I set something up with Judy. She'll be such a good sounding board for you," Mom says.

Judy is Mom's psychiatrist friend. I love Judy to bits, I really do. But the last thing I want to do is get "shrinked." Shrunk?

"No Judy, but thanks." I stare at the vegetables sizzling on the stove.

"Sweetie—"

I put my hand out. "Mom, stop. You're suffocating me. Could you just trust me to work through this on my own?"

By the look on her face, I can tell she's practically biting her tongue. Nods. "Set the table for me?"

"Why you not eating chicken, Claire? You l-l-love meat. You do," Belle says.

"Belle, you know I don't eat meat."

"Nothing with a face, right?"

"Right, Belle." I scoop up some vegetables with chickpeas and cashews Mom made just for me.

"I never did hear what the deciding factor was for you to become a vegetarian," Dad says as he forks a piece of zucchini.

"Reading books and articles about the food industry, watching documentaries like *Earthlings* and *Food Inc.*, contemplating the sorry state of our planet. Cow farts alone affect climate change more than the pollution from cars."

"How do you measure a cow fart, anyway?" Dad says, smiling.

Belle giggles. "Daddy said f-f-fart. He said fart." There's mushed-up rice in her open mouth.

"Each cow produces more than ten kilos of methane gas every year. Multiply that by about a bazillion cows in Saskatchewan alone," I say.

"Do chickens fart?" Mom asks.

Belle's now laughing so hard her chewed-up food plops on her plate.

"Belle, food stays in your mouth," Mom says, laughing herself as she hands Belle a napkin.

"This is serious," I say. "You're the Buddhist, Dad. How do you justify eating animals?"

"I'm not cruel to animals."

"Eating them isn't being cruel?"

"When the Dalai Lama was asked why he eats chicken, he said, 'Because I'm not a strict Buddhist.'" Dad is obviously trying to be funny.

"What a cop-out," I say.

Dad winces. There's a thin film over his feelings and I hate it when it gets pierced. Hate it even more when I've done the piercing.

There's a long silence as we all continue to eat. I glance up. Dad still looks hurt. I'm desperate to smooth things over with him. "Can we paint tonight?"

He doesn't look so sure.

"Great idea," Mom says, glancing over at him.

"Yeah, m-m-me, too, Daddy. I want to paint. I do. I do, too."

"Bath tonight, Belle," Mom says. "You can paint with

Dad another time."

Belle makes a wailing sound like a vacuum motor ready to conk out.

Dad's studio is a psychedelic temple. His paintings are filled with bold strokes of bright colors and abstract shapes that look like ghosts ready to leap out of the canvas. Most of his paintings take up whole walls in the studio, and in offices and monster homes in cities all over North America. Some have even made their way to Europe. There are large windows and a skylight in the studio, so natural light pours in from everywhere. In one corner, Dad has a small shrine with a pillow on the floor, where he meditates a couple of times a day. Beside the meditation cushion is an altar with a teak statue of Buddha and a framed calligraphy painting by a Rinpoche, a Tibetan teacher.

I like watching Dad paint. He stands back from his enormous canvas and just stares at the first few strokes of paint for an uncomfortably long time. He reminds me of a diver who waits for what seems like an eternity, visualizing the dive before taking the plunge off a platform the height of a small building. I think Dad channels the art gods. When he finally daubs some paint in a blank corner, it means the vision has come to him. After that, it's like a flurry of color and movement—his own acrobatic routine moving from one side of the canvas to another. Because the paintings are so big, he has a small lift, like the ones used to repair streetlights, so he can reach the high spots.

My space in the studio has a few easels and all the canvases and paint I want. I love the smell of paint, love mixing colors to create new ones. Love the terrifying but exhilarating feeling of painting the first brush stroke on a blank canvas. Since kindergarten, my art teachers have told me I have a knack for painting, that I've inherited my father's artistic genes. When I was in Grade 2, the mayor of Vancouver toured our school. Our gift to him for pretending he was interested in the state of elementary education in the city was a picture I painted of my school, the roofline all wonky and the kids in the playground looking like mutant amphibians. He was voted out the next year so he probably chucked it. Then I came fourth in a city-wide art competition in Grade 9. I'm really proud of that painting.

A girl sitting on a branch of a tree, looking up at the sky. Sunlight streaming through the branches, the pattern on the leaves, the girl's flowing blonde hair, the texture of the tree bark. Dad said he liked it but challenged me to push my painting further. Experiment. Take more risks. I still have so much to learn.

When he and I paint in the studio together, it's usually painfully quiet for me. He occasionally glances over at my work, but only comments, encourages, or makes suggestions when we're done for the day. He's thrifty with words at the best of times, as if there's a tax on speaking. *Mr. Winters, that 26-word sentence you just spoke will cost you $9.62. Please pay the cashier.* When he paints, it's like he's taken a vow of silence. But not tonight. He doesn't even pick up a brush. Instead, he sits on a table beside me and nervously pulls on his ear. This is one of his strange little quirks—a sure sign he's trying to compose an awkward sentence in his mind.

I inspect my unfinished portraits of Butch, Jimmy, and Trudy, people who live in the Downtown Eastside, one of the poorest postal codes in the country. I want to donate these portraits to a silent auction for the Neighborhood House, the place where my mom sometimes helps out. I put the portrait of Butch on the easel in front of me, but all my mind will register is a slideshow of the photos I took of Will on the bridge. I give my head a shake and grab a new canvas instead.

Dad's making me nervous just sitting there.

"Let me guess ... Mom wants me to spill my guts to you about the guy on the bridge?"

"Pretty much. How you doing?"

"Do I look all freaked out?" I mix Payne's gray, burnt sienna, and permanent green together into a dark mud.

"Not any more than usual." He cracks a smile, a good sign.

"Thanks."

"Your mom and I care very much, that's all."

"I know. And I do appreciate it, but ..."

I daub my brush into the paint and twirl it on the white canvas to create a grubby galaxy of stars, planets, and asteroids. "Dad?"

"Yeah." He swings his legs.

"Do Buddhists believe in Hell?"

Dad lets out a big sigh and gives his ear another tug.

"Buddhists believe it's one realm of existence."

"Do you believe that people go to Hell for killing themselves?"

"I guess it depends on the circumstance."

"Like what?"

"Well," there goes the ear tug again, "if a person was in extreme physical or mental pain, or if they killed themselves to save others ..."

"You mean, if a soldier was being tortured by the enemy and ate cyanide instead of revealing the whereabouts of his platoon?"

"Something like that."

"What if a person's girlfriend broke up with him, or he lost his job, or was just tired of living on this Earth?"

"Well, as you brought up at dinner, the first teaching in Buddhism is to not harm living things. That includes yourself."

"Where's his soul? The jumper's, I mean."

"No idea, Claire."

"I hope he doesn't go to Hell."

Dad nods. I daub my paintbrush into a squirt of cadmium yellow and brush a tiny bright star in the stormy star cluster. It's all I'm inspired to paint and that scares the hell out of me.

"My muse is missing in action," I say and put down my paintbrush.

"That happens sometimes." Dad slides off the table, walks over behind me. He rests his warm hand on my shoulder, and I realize how rarely we touch anymore.

Lying in bed, my body aches for sleep, but my brain continues riffing in high gear. Is Will burning in Hell with all the mass murderers, terrorists, corrupt politicians, and environmental polluters? Or is he in Heaven, wearing a long, flowing white robe and strumming a harp as angels flap their wings around him, feeding him peeled grapes? Maybe he's in some holding tank for people who commit suicide. How does God (if there actually is a God) deal with people who were given the gift of life, but chose to give it back? Is suicide an unforgiveable sin?

One thing that got me up every morning ... One thing that I was good at, and gave me hope for my future. When that was taken away, there wasn't much left to hang around for.

The one thing that's important to me. The one thing I'm good at. The one thing that gives me hope for my future. I turn on my bedside lamp, grab my sketchbook and pencil, and flip to a blank page. I stare at the page for what seems like eons, trying to conjure a flash of creativity. *Nada.* I put pencil to paper to try to get some flow going, but the tip snaps in two.

Chapter 8

I duck aside as Izzy charges into the kitchen, carrying a tray of dirty dishes. "Holy geez. It's been so freakin' busy all morning." The dishes clank in the sink. "Where are all these people coming from?" She looks her wonderfully bizarre self—drowning in a men's XL Hawaiian shirt tucked into a shocking-pink mini-skirt and knee-high white Doc Martens. It's enough to hurt your eyes first thing in the morning.

I tie up my apron, ready to start my shift, but I'm exhausted. I woke up several times in the night from the same dream—Will jumped off the bridge and I followed right behind him. Sometimes we held hands and jumped together. The wind resisted our fall but gravity always won. I kept waking up just before I landed in the water.

Remembering the dream, my body starts to shake and I'm drenched in sweat.

"You look like you just saw a ghost or something," Izzy says.

I go down the hallway into the tiny staff bathroom, shut the door, tie my hair into a knot, and splash water on my face. I flop down on the toilet seat and stare at the hand-painted sign left by the previous owners—*Yellow is mellow; if it's brown, flush it down.* I come out of the bathroom and Tessa's waiting for me. Ty must have told her about the jumper because she wraps me in a big hug. "You don't have to be here, you know. I can call Celia. We'll manage." I rest my head on her shoulder, my face in her long, graying, cotton candy hair that smells like mangoes.

"I'll be fine ... just fine," I say. After a while, I stop shaking.

The shiny steel machine spews out the last drop of espresso into a tiny cup. I load it onto a tray along with a pot of Peach Passion tea and take it to Archie and Maggie, two of our regulars.

"Twenty six down—a muse. Five letters," Archie says. Archie and Maggie meet most days at the cc to do the crossword together or discuss books and poetry. Archie is a seventy-one-year-old retired professor. Tessa thinks he's a dead ringer for Robert Redford, an old movie star. All I know is he's the only man I know who is that old and can dress like a beach dude in boarder shorts and funky T-shirts without looking like a poser.

"A muse. What's it start with?"

"E."

Maggie thinks for a moment. "Erato?"

"One of the Greek muses. Must be right. Well done, Maggie," says Archie as he writes it down.

I put down the tray and hand Archie his espresso and Maggie her tea. A few months back, Maggie, a twenty-three-year-old single mom, glommed onto Archie when she overheard him talking about a book they had both read. She was in university, majoring in literature, but had to drop out when she had her baby.

"Forty-two across … oh, dear, you'll have to help us out with this one, Claire. Which Canadian band includes the mandolin, French horn, and hurdy-gurdy in their music?"

Bruin, Maggie's eight-month-old baby, starts fussing, so Maggie pops out her doughy boob and lets him feed. The kid must be addicted to Peach Passion tea.

"Arcade Fire?" Izzy and I are usually the go-to people for contemporary music clues.

"Yes, that fits. Thank you, my dear. Twenty-eight down ..." says Archie.

The Cosmic Cow Café has been a Kitsilano landmark since the 1970s. Tessa took it over in 2014 and kept the decor. People have been known to drive all the way from Abbotsford for Tessa's famous Magic Mushroom burgers (non-hallucinogenic), the Nirvana artichoke and goat cheese salad, the organic sorbets, frozen yogurts, and smoothies called Moo-thies. Posters of old rock and roll bands like the Grateful Dead, The Doors, and The Rolling Stones hang on the walls, along with black and white photos of a music festival Archie told me about called Woodstock. Classic rock and roll music blares out the speakers. From what Archie told me about the hippie movement in the 60s and 70s—sex, drugs, and rock and roll—it's so not

Tessa. She reminds me of a librarian or church choir leader. Never smoked pot in her whole life—she's never even smoked cigarettes. She only drinks Scotch on special occasions and, although she likes all kinds of music, she prefers Mozart to Mick Jagger.

I clear the table where Izzy is on a break. Ellie, another CC regular, reads Izzy's tea leaves.

"Well, isn't this interesting," says Ellie as she peers through her thick reading glasses into Izzy's cup. "There's a hand and it's pointing to an anchor." Ellie just had her ninety-third birthday. Her bright orange lipstick is usually smudged at the sides of her mouth, and she dresses all fancy-like in pastel suits, stockings that bag at her knees, and white shoes.

"An anchor. What's that mean?" Izzy asks all excited.

"That you have good and loyal friends," Ellie says.

Izzy grabs my arm, almost knocking over the tray of dishes. "You got that right, Ellie." She pulls me down and gives me a peck on the cheek.

"It also means you will find an enduring love one day," Ellie says.

"Aces," says Izzy, a bit too loudly. "Any idea when I'll meet my love?"

"The tea leaves aren't clear on that," says Ellie.

I carry the tray to the next table. There it is. The Classified section of the *Vancouver Sun* open to the page with Will's obituary. There's a small photo of him. He looks so happy. So alive.

WILLIAM (WILL) JOSEF SZABO. It is with great sadness that we announce the sudden and tragic passing of our beloved Will at the age of twenty. He is survived by his mother, Patricia, and his sister Lauren (Vancouver), and father, Peter (Montreal). Will was a shining light in our hearts who touched many people in his short life. He will be greatly missed by everyone who knew him. The service will be held 2:00 PM, Friday, July 15th at Holy Trinity Orthodox Church.

Father lives in Montreal (parents obviously divorced), but his mother and sister live here in Vancouver. I suddenly have an overwhelming desire to meet them.

As if on cue—enter stage left—he walks into the café. The brown suit from the bridge. I'll never forget his thin beak nose. He's wearing a black suit today. On the bridge, he just appeared beside me, speechless. His forehead folded into waves of shock when he realized Will had actually jumped. He looks around the café as if he's arrived at the wrong costume party, sits at a small table, and skims the menu. My feet move without me and I end up at his table. He glances up. The rough ridges of his cheeks look like someone slapped clay on his face and sculpted it with a trowel.

"I would like the Leo the Lion lentil soup, please," he says. "Does that come with rye bread?"

My tongue won't work but my brain starts spinning. In his suit and maroon and white striped tie, he looks like some actor from an old black and white movie I saw at the Vogue Theater, where everyone chain-smoked and talked like they were reading from a dictionary, and where men and women slept in separate beds, and a kiss was as far as they could go (no tongues allowed), and everyone drove in their funny convertibles, scarves sailing in the fake wind because the cars weren't really moving but the scenery behind them was, and they would drive off into a shrinking tiny circle, while an out-of-tune band played and *The End* appeared on the blank screen.

He looks confused when I sit down across from him. "Oh, excuse me. I thought you worked here. Is this your table?"

"Yes. Well, no. It belongs to the café." I'm so lame.

"I'm sorry." He pushes away from the table and stands.

"Please don't. Leave, I mean." My tongue takes over from my feet, but my brain is still riffing. What am I doing? He gazes at me from the corner of his eye like I'm some psycho, but he slowly sinks back down into the chair. His forehead crinkles.

"I was there, too," I finally blurt out. "At the bridge. The Lions Gate."

"Oh, I see." He looks out the window, his jittery fingers tap-tap-tapping on the table. "Tragic. So very tragic."

"Yeah, I've been thinking the same thing."

Just then, Ty and Declan charge into the café, making more racket than a football team that just won the big game. Declan picks up Bruin from Maggie's lap and throws him over his shoulder. The kid squeals like a happy piglet. Ty comes to the table and looks at the suit like he's a freaky statue.

"Hey," Ty says.

"Hey," I answer.

"You're done working, right?"

I wish he would go away. "I have a few minutes left."

"Still coming to the protest with us?" Ty asks me. Then looks at the man. "Pipelines, oil tankers ..."

The suit checks the time on his cellphone and stands up. "Here, take my seat," he says to Ty.

"What about your soup?" I ask.

"Not to worry. I'll take lunch with me."

He digs into his pocket, pulls out his business card, and puts it on the table in front of me. Our eyes lock for a second or two. I can tell he wishes I hadn't ruined his day. He heads for the counter where Tessa greets him.

Ty sits down in the suit's chair. I read the business card.

Bernard Oswald, CA, Managing Partner

Oswald and Associates, Chartered Accountants

Tax Planning and Management Consulting

His phone number, office address downtown, and email are across the bottom.

"Was gramps trying to pick you up or something?" Ty smirks.

"Don't be a jerk." I sound bitchier than I want, but it seems to roll off Ty.

Why did Bernard give me his card? Is he as messed up about Will as I am? Does he need to talk to me about the jumper as much as I need to talk to him?

Izzy comes to the table and pulls on my arm. "Your turn. Ellie's already poured you a cup of tea."

"Not feelin' it today."

On a normal day, I would be all over it. Ellie has been freakishly accurate in some of her readings. Like when she saw a heart in Tessa's cup. Ellie told her she would meet a new love and then described Celia in detail—right down to the cowboy boots she likes to wear. And when there was the shape of a key in Maggie's tea leaves, Ellie told

Maggie that she would have to move from her apartment. A month later, Maggie got notice; a developer had bought the building and was turning it into condos.

"Come on, Claire. The tea leaves made the shape of a bird in my cup. Ellie told me that means my psychic powers will be sharpened." Izzy taps her forehead. "She also saw a grasshopper, which means a friend will be joining the military."

"Don't look at me." Ty holds up his hands as if he's surrendering.

I stand. "I've got to finish the dishes before I leave." I clear a table on the way to the counter.

"I can help." He follows me, grabs a few dirty dishes off other tables, and loads up my tray.

"No, but thanks anyway." My head is spinning. I need to hide in the kitchen, alone, and try to untangle my thoughts about meeting Bernard—the brown suit from the bridge.

"I'll wait for you," Ty says.

"You're not going anywhere, buster, until you hug your momma," Tessa says.

He picks Tessa up, right off the ground, and spins her

around like they're in pairs figure skating. He sets her down, reaches behind the counter and grabs a wrapped sandwich out of the cooler, gestures to Declan, and throws it to him. Tessa hands Ty a few cookies.

Balancing my full tray, I push through the swinging door into the quiet kitchen.

Chapter 9

At English Bay Beach, gray clouds roll across the sky and block the sun. Izzy, Declan, Ty, and I stand with the dozens of people protesting the proposed pipeline expansion and oil tanker traffic that could pollute our water. I spot a few other Earth Rescue members sprinkled in the crowd. People hold signs and shout out slogans like, "System change, not climate change," "No pipelines, no tankers," and "Protect our ocean." A large inflatable Orca hovers over the crowd. A group of Indigenous people are drumming and singing. Some wear ceremonial red capes and woven cedar hats. Izzy holds up her homemade sign—*We Are Making Waves for an Oil-free Coast*. People who support the pipelines are holding up signs like *Energy brings jobs, Support*

Pipeline Expansion, and *I Love Canadian Oil & Gas*. One person calls out, "I need a job. The energy economy and environment can coexist." I want to shout back at him, "But at what cost?" Instead I keep my mouth shut.

One of the protest organizers stands on a chair, speaks into a microphone, and welcomes the crowd. She wears a white T-shirt that reads: *There is No Planet B*.

"If this pipeline expansion is approved, it will mean seven times the tanker traffic through the Burrard Inlet. This will increase the risk of spills in the water off our densely populated communities. We need to unite with one voice to stop the possible degradation of our waterways." Protesters clap and cheer, while those opposed shout their disapproval.

"As a marine biologist, I know only too well the devastating effects of oil spills on marine birds and mammals, as well as fish and shellfish," she says. "Specifically, oil destroys the insulating capability of fur-bearing mammals such as sea otters, as well as the ability for birds to repel water. If oil is leaked into our coastal waters, this means birds and mammals could die from hypothermia."

She goes on to talk about the effects of oil on fish and shellfish, including enlarged livers, fin erosion, and changes in heart rates. I'm seriously distracted and only hear the odd word from the other speaker, who talks about Canada not meeting emissions targets, and how Indigenous peoples' rights have been ignored. I thought attending this protest on saving the ocean—something I'm passionate about—would distract me. But it hasn't. I can't get rid of the image of Will's body floating in a filmy pool of oil leaked from a tanker, alongside dead otters, fish, and seabirds.

Enormous apartment buildings tower over us as we weave through the West End streets to where Ty parked the van.

"Oh, guys, I forgot to tell you something." Izzy's eyes light up. She loves to be the holder of secrets and stories no one has heard. Or weird anecdotes, such as male seahorses giving their partners a hug every morning during pregnancy, a guy faking his death to get out of paying off his cellphone contract, and human hearts beating over 100,000 times a day. "An old boyfriend of my aunt knows the family of that guy."

"What guy?" Ty says, kicking a pinecone down the sidewalk.

"The Lions Gate jumper guy—who else, silly?"

Will, floating in the oil slick, is etched into my mind. I feel sick.

"Can we please just change the subject?" Ty says.

But Izzy doesn't stop for a breath, even when Ty runs his finger across his throat and sticks his tongue way out for emphasis.

"Apparently, relatives are coming to the funeral all the way from Serbia or Hungaria, or someplace like that," says Izzy.

"Hungary?" Declan says.

"Not really," Izzy says.

Ty and Declan crack up laughing. Izzy has a puzzled look. Declan goes back to thumbing through his cellphone.

Now the words from Will's suicide note swarm my mind.

People are going to say I'm selfish for killing myself when I have family and friends who love me. But they don't understand.

Izzy turns to me. "Are you going to the funeral?"

"Why would I go? I didn't even know the guy." Of course I'm going to Will's funeral.

"Maybe it would help you ... you know ..." Ty says, kicking the same pinecone.

"Help me what?" I ask.

"It's just that ..." he looks around like he's trying to find the words in the air.

Declan jumps in. "You've always admitted to being more morose than the average teenager—right, Claire? Well, lately, you've dialed it up a notch ... you know ... since ..."

I turn to Izzy. "Have I really been that moody?" I was hoping no one had noticed.

Izzy turns to me, gets into my face, so close she looks like a cyclops. "You know we love you. But yes, Claire, you have been moodier lately. And for good reason, I might add." She leans away. "I heard this therapist on a talk show who believes in talk therapy, and she interviewed all these people who experienced traumatic events like tornados, hijackings, 9/11 ... One guy was trapped in his car for six straight days, living on drips of rain that came through a crack in the window. Each of them went through talk therapy; they may have been medicated a little bit, too, but—"

"We get it, Izzy," Ty says.

A clump of Izzy's bleached bangs slumps over her face.

"I'm hardly the only one who gets moody," I say to Declan. "What about when you only got 82% on your essay, "Nuclear Weapons—Global Peacemakers or Killing Devices"? You sulked for days." Declan shrugs, nods in agreement. I turn to Izzy. "And when the vintage clothing store by your place shut down, you locked yourself in your room for a whole weekend. And Ty, when someone scooped up that free washing machine you wanted to repair and then sell for three hundred bucks, no one wanted to be around you for at least a day."

I take a breath while they digest my tirade. "I don't need therapy, for crying out loud," I say. Softer, "Trust me, all is well in my world." My queasy stomach says differently.

We walk quietly for a few blocks until we reach the van.

"If all is well, Claire, then you don't mind hearing some famous last words?" Declan says, holding up his phone.

"Of course not." I try to sound convincing. Swallow hard.

"You're sure?" Declan says. "I don't want to provoke any more trauma."

"Yes, I'm sure. For cripes sake!" I am not sure at all.

Ty unlocks the van doors. Izzy and Declan pile into the back seat.

Ty starts the van and pulls out.

"Here goes." Declan reads Kurt Cobain's suicide note, with feeling. "'Frances and Courtney, I'll be at your altar. Please keep going, Courtney, for Frances, for her life will be so much happier without me. I LOVE YOU. I LOVE YOU.'"

"Rest in peace, my man," Ty says.

"Russian poet Sergei blah-biddy-blah wrote, 'Goodbye everybody' in his own blood, gave the note to a friend, and then hung himself," Declan says.

"I think that's romantic," says Izzy.

"You would," Ty says.

Darkness washes over me as we drive through the downtown traffic. Guess I wasn't ready for this, after all.

"Oh, this one ... Some newscaster shot herself on the evening news. Right before, she said, 'Always bringing you the latest in blood and guts, in living color, you're about to see another first—an attempted suicide.' She pointed the gun behind her right ear."

"Gross. Brains splattered all over the place," says Ty. "And during the dinner hour, too."

I start to feel sick to my stomach.

"Did she die?" Izzy asks.

"In the hospital, fourteen hours later," Declan says.

Is Will's suicide note going to be plastered all over WhatsApp, Snapchat, and Twitter? Makes me want to keep his cellphone forever and not tell a soul.

One thing that I was good at and gave me hope for my future. When that was taken away, there wasn't much left to hang around for ... I would have been a useless piece of shit if I just kept living my life like an empty shell.

"Let me out," I say to Ty, reaching for the door handle.

"What? Here?" he says.

"Yeah, pull over anywhere."

Ty sighs loudly. Looks in his rearview and makes a face at Declan. When he pulls over, I grab my purse.

"Want me to come with you, sweetie?" Izzy asks.

"No, but thanks." I open the door.

"Text me. I'll pick you up later," Ty says.

"I'll just take the bus. See you." I shut the door. Can't seem to control my crazy moodiness. If they didn't already have enough evidence, I just confirmed to my friends that I am a certifiable nut bar. I join the swarm on the sidewalk, moving in the opposite direction.

Although it's almost closing time at the Vancouver Art Gallery, I enter anyway. Worth it even for a half hour, thanks to the annual pass my dad gives me every year for Christmas.

I walk straight to the Emily Carr Collection—she's one of my favorite artists. I often come here for inspiration. Or when I feel particularly depressed and want to disappear forever into one of her paintings. It's quiet. I'm the only one here. I sit on the wooden bench and take in the enchanting forests—the contrasting colors when light peeks through the trees, the movement of the swirling lines, the brooding clouds, cubist funnels of light. Words that pop into my mind: form ... connection ... roots ... silence. There's a scrunched-up piece of paper on the polished wooden floor. I pick it up and smooth out the creases. Someone wrote this:

The Liveness in me just loves to feel the
liveness in growing things, in grass and rain
and leaves and flowers...
~ Emily Carr

I fold the note and put it into my purse. I walk around the room and see paintings of Indigenous villages, landscapes, and Carr's signature crazy trees. I come to the painting titled *Vanquished* that I've seen many times before. It's of a deserted village, tipped-over totem poles, coffins made out of cedars. Isolation ... desolation ... ruin ... death. I came here to find peace, but this painting makes me feel gutted. The tears start, and there's nothing I can do to stop them.

Chapter 10

It's dawn. I wake up from a dream that I was being chased through an Emily Carr-like forest; a strong wind that sounded like high-pitched screams whistled through the whirly trees. As I was running, I could barely catch my breath—kept tripping over dead logs, ending with a face-plant in the cold soil.

I pick up my book of poems by Emily Dickinson from the bedside table. It randomly opens to "Grief is a Mouse." Grief is described as being a thief and a juggler, sneaky and furtive. The last stanza reads:

Best Grief is Tongueless — before He'll tell —
Burn Him in the Public Square —

His Ashes — will

Possibly — if they refuse — How then know —

Since a Rack couldn't coax a syllable — now.

"Tongueless." Not talked about because there's nothing to say. Grief never rests. Although it's hidden away, it weighs on a person, is felt so deeply. I close the book and try to go back to sleep.

My body and brain start an all-out war—my body's begging for sleep, but my brain turns on the ignition and revs into high gear. I dig in my drawer and find Will's cellphone. Decide to check his email. Mostly spam from airlines, sports magazines, and several Interac e-Transfer notices from Patricia Szabo—his mother, according to Will's obituary. No cash sent from his father in Montreal.

I'm in deep now, so I creep Will's Instagram account.

His handle is WillZa.

#soccer #instafutbol #score #fifa #realmadrid #worldcup #beer #morebeer

163 posts

394 followers

93 following

Other than a smattering of rock-climbing, snow-boarding, and beer-guzzling photos, most are about soccer, soccer, and more soccer.

Will in front of the net, his leg reaching back, ready to kick the ball in front of him.

Don't go through life without goals. Get it, team?

JaketheSnake: *Got it.*

SerenaBella: *Lame*

DaveP: **Groan**

55 Likes

Will chasing the ball, an opponent running alongside him.

The scouts are out! Coach says I'm being watched ... closely.

IMDanny: *So proud of you, babe!*

beekyzoom: *Awww ...*

JJBeano: *Way to go, bud.*

189 Likes

Four pics of Will and his girlfriend outside Has Bean coffee shop.

Best java in the whole city. And right around the corner from home—385 steps to be exact. Beauty!

42 likes

Last post from Will was about five months before he killed himself. He must have just scored the winning goal. In the photo, he has a huge, gorgeous smile, his brown hair pasted to his sweaty face.

Should hear about the scholarship by the end of the month. South Carolina—here I come!

flyboy67: *They'd be crazy not to take you*

Creatureofcomfort: *Good job, bro*

Twenty-five more congratulatory comments.

203 likes

Was that it? He didn't get a soccer scholarship so his life wasn't worth living?

Will's face crowds my mind, invades my dreams constantly. I haven't looked at the photos I took of him on the bridge. I pick up my phone, open my photos. But I'm not quite ready.

When I finally make my way downstairs, Mom and Dad are putting on their coats and pouring coffee into their travel mugs.

"Where you going?" I ask.

"Langley," Mom says.

"Why?"

"Don't you remember? We discussed this at dinner the other night," Dad says.

"Um ... kind of. What's going on again?"

"There's a new program we want to check out for Belle," Dad says.

"They offer more structure than Belle's getting now," Mom chimes in. "More work and life skills training."

"Work? Belle?"

"She's capable of many things. This might help her figure out exactly what," Dad says, then calls out to Belle. "TV off, Bella-Belle. Time to go."

I ride down Cornwall Avenue to Burrard Street, but get off

my bike before I cross the Burrard Bridge. My hands and feet tingle and my stomach flip-flops. I close my eyes and try to visualize myself cycling over the bridge, but it just makes me light-headed. I muster every ounce of oomph I have, hop back on my bike, and ride as fast as I can, dodging other cyclists, walkers, and skateboarders. Could have sworn I saw Will peering over the edge of the railing, but I zoom right by. My stomach starts to heave the closer I get to the other side of the bridge. I make it across to Pacific Street, jump off my bike while the wheels are still turning, and puke on a small patch of grass while people stroll by, looking thoroughly grossed out. Will I never be able to cross a bridge again in my life without feeling sick to my stomach?

"As I mentioned to you, it was a tragic event." Bernie leans forward, his elbows resting on his silky black trousers. Over email, I'd arranged to meet Bernard Oswald. He suggested we talk in the foyer of his downtown office building. We both saw Will "off" himself. I am sure Bernie's the only one who will truly understand the breath-crushing weight on my body. My zero concentration. My warped reality.

"Such wasted potential." His cellphone bleeps on the table in front of us.

"Wasted potential?" I'm crushed.

"From the newspaper report, he seemed to be a vibrant young man with a promising future." Bernie nods at someone who's leaving the building.

"Doesn't it play over and over again for you? Will walking across the bridge like he doesn't have a care in the world, then, a moment later, you and I are leaning over the railing, staring into the ocean."

"Yes, I've often thought about that day." He looks seriously uncomfortable, glances at the text message on his phone. "I'm not quite sure what it is you want from me, Claire."

I shrug, look out the enormously tall windows at the bustle of suits with cellphones growing out of their ears. "I was hoping you would know."

"Not everything has an answer, I'm afraid. Things happen that are beyond our comprehension." His foot taps nervously.

His words of wisdom are about as profound as an infomercial for a funeral home. But what was I expecting from Bernie? Did I think we would somehow bond over our shared experience?

"That's it?" I raise my voice. "But how do you make sense of it, Mr. Oswald? Will Szabo killed himself right in front of us." My face is hot. "Don't you wonder what was going on for him? Why he lost hope? Don't you ever think we could have stopped him, somehow, from jumping?"

Bernie looks around to see if anyone overheard me, sighs, shakes his head, and stares at his shiny black shoes. "I was quite a way past when it happened, I'm afraid."

I rewind my memory to that day. Will on his phone. He laughs. Bernie had already walked past us. He turned around when Will laughed, kept walking.

"But I was right there. I even touched him. I touched his white shirt." I stick my thumb nail into my tingling fingertip.

"I can't imagine there was any way to stop that young man. He seemed determined."

"So that's it?"

Bernie's probably been on this Earth about thirty years

longer than me. Isn't he supposed to have some wisdom about life and death stuff?

"I'm not sure what else I can do for you." He just stares at me for several seconds, probably trying to figure out how to get rid of me. He looks over at the security guard sitting at the reception desk. He digs his wallet out of his back pocket. "You may want to contact a client of mine." He unfolds his wallet and pulls out one of the loose pieces of paper stuck inside. Hands it to me. "He deals with these kinds of situations." The paper reads: *Paul Couvelier.* The paper has lines that fold together—like in a kid's activity book. This is a business card?

"Is he some kind of priest or shrink?"

"Both, in a matter of speaking. Paul might be someone you would find interesting to talk to. My apologies, but I do have to rush to a meeting," he says as he stands up. "I hope you find the answers you're looking for, Claire. I really do."

"Thanks." *For nothing,* I say with my inside voice. He checks his phone one more time as he heads to the elevator. What was I expecting from Bernie?

I feel faint and queasy at the thought of riding back over the bridge. And the security guard keeps looking over at me, which makes me nervous. I check my handbag for bus fare or cab money, but I left my wallet at home. I wish I'd asked to borrow some cash from Bernie. I want to call my parents but they're with Belle in Langley. I feel so alone.

I look closely at Paul Couvelier's "card." St. Michael's Hospice Society. On my phone I search: *What is a hospice?* Find out it's a home that provides care for the sick or terminally ill. I fold the lines on the card and it turns into a tiny origami robot. Who is this weird Paul guy?

I lock up my bike near the front door of the hospice and stuff my helmet in my handbag. St. Michael's is a lot like the Strathcona neighborhood where it lives. Pots of flowers outside the front door try their best to brighten things up, but the patches on the stonework can't hide the age of the building.

St. Michael's inside is like finding a tropical paradise in the middle of a desert. The foyer has a glass ceiling that lets in light for real trees, including a palm tree, and many flowering plants. A small waterfall trickles gently. But the amazing thing is three cages of colorful, exotic-looking birds, also alive and real. Reminds me of the Amazon Rainforest I learned about in a documentary.

I have no idea what Paul does here at the hospice. Did Bernie say he was a priest or something? Anyone who has an origami-robot business card can't be that hardcore religious. Or, at the least, he must have a hardcore sense of humor. I approach a man who looks like he knows his way around.

"Can I help you?" he says.

"I'm looking for Paul Couvelier." The guy doesn't even blink, so I guess I didn't totally slaughter Paul's last name.

"His office is at the end of the hall to the left."

I walk further down the hallway where a man is talking to a female nurse. He's short with a head of curly brown hair, and his bushy eyebrows are dangerously at risk of joining forces and becoming a unibrow.

"Paul Couvelier?"

"Yes, and you are ...?"

"Claire Winters."

"No time for the volunteer orientation right now, but how about you just start reading to Mr. Wells in room 12. And call him Tommy—he hates formality." Paul walks briskly down the hallway, obviously in a big hurry.

"Hi, I'm Sandy," the nurse says. "His room is that way." She points in the opposite direction from where Paul went. "Tommy can seem a bit gruff—he's not exactly happy to be here. But he's a sweet man, once you get to know him."

"Actually, I'm not here to volunteer. I'm just here to talk to Paul," I say.

"Oh, well," she says. "Today is crazy for Paul. But if you don't mind hanging around, he might be able to squeeze you in."

"Thanks."

Perfect opportunity to snoop around. The hospice has very tasteful artwork, most of it donated by local artists, according to the plaques. I particularly like one landscape with puffy clouds and gray sky taking up most of the painting, with only a small line of rolling hills and trees stretching across the bottom. Another painting is of an old-character house with funky shapes and bright colors. In a tiny top floor window a Tabby cat peeks out. Down another hall I recognize an abstract painting. Dad's. The muted colors and geometric shapes seem to fit well in a hospice. Nothing tangible that you can touch—just shadowy and dreamlike.

A wooden sculpture of an angel sits on a table in a bright window, around it small cards with names and messages. I lean in to read them: Olivia Reed – *I will love you forever, Mom.* Clint Jones – *We will miss you, Dad.* Jody Livingston – *You always have a place in my heart.* Messages to their loved ones who died. My heart feels tied in a knot. I continue exploring.

Down the hall, I walk by a bedroom. A boy about eleven, tubes coming out his nose, is hooked up to machines that are pumping and sighing. He's playing a video game.

I keep walking until I come to a room with a big-screen TV, a stereo, bookshelves, and a small kitchen area. A pale, bald, super-thin woman sits in a puffy leather chair with two little girls cuddled up on either side of her. One of the girls strokes the bald woman's cheek while a man leans against the windowsill, reading aloud from a children's book.

A golden retriever bounds down the hallway toward me. "Elvis, chill out." A girl about my age follows Elvis, her bald head covered by a baseball cap that says: *In dog years, I'm dead*. She says, "Don't worry, he's a big suck." An understatement. Elvis's tail is wagging like a metronome on high speed, and he leans right into me while I pat him.

"I didn't know dogs were allowed in hospitals," I say.

"Welcome to hospice. It's like a different planet here."

"Is he your dog?"

"Belongs to one of the nurses, but I must have a dog pheromone or something because he follows me around everywhere. I'm Kiki, by the way."

"Claire."

"What brings you to hospice?" Kiki has charcoal circles under her eyes and I can almost see her veins pumping blood just under the surface of her see-through skin. She has no eyelashes and her eyebrows are drawn with a pencil.

"I'm hoping to talk to Paul Couvelier."

"Mr. Hospice himself. Good luck—he's as busy as a one-legged man in an ass-kicking competition. Just heading out for a smoke. Wanna come?"

She leads me to a small outdoor patio. Elvis follows. We sit down in the two rickety white plastic chairs with an ashtray stand between us. Elvis flops down right beside Kiki and rests his head on her foot. "I started smoking last year," she says. "I thought, what the hell? I'm dying anyway." She offers me a cigarette.

"No, thanks, don't smoke."

"It is a dirty habit, but what the hell?"

She lights her cigarette between her purple lips, takes a long drag.

"My doctor isn't a believer in medical marijuana. Really pisses me off. I mean, he'll pump me with morphine or oxycodone like it's running out of style—and I'm not complaining, it's pretty fantabulous—but it knocks me on my ass. I'd like to be more awake, or reasonably awake, or at least just a little bit less stoned for whatever time I have left." She's so matter-of-fact it makes me uncomfortable. Like she's talking about how much of summer holidays she has left. She takes another drag.

"How long have you been here?" I ask.

"It's not as if I live at hospice—I'm not waiting to

breathe my last breath or anything. Whenever my mom needs a break, she drops me off here. The alternative is the hospital. Barf. I'd either end up on a ward with all the wrinkly old people who reek of piss, or they'd put me in the children's ward. Being with sick kids breaks my heart."

Seeing how skinny and pale Kiki is breaks *my* heart. "But people here are dying," I say.

"Yeah, just like me. As they say, we're all dying, right?" She takes another drag. "Not really supposed to use hospice as a hotel, but Paul has a soft spot for me. The feeling's mutual. My mom and I moved here a few months ago from Fort Nelson to be closer to the cancer clinic—and now hospice, I guess. We don't have any family here and the few friends my mom has are afraid I'll die on them." She coughs as she exhales a puff of smoke. "I don't blame my mom or anything. She doesn't handle stress all that well, and since my tumor had babies, I haven't exactly been a shitload of giggles." She inhales, coughs again. "Time for meds. Better get going." Kiki stubs out her cigarette in the ashtray and hands me her cellphone. "Put your number in my phone. Promise I'm not some weirdo stalker, but I hardly know anyone my age in this city. Hospice will be my home base for a few weeks, so maybe we can hang out sometime."

"Sure, give me a call." I put in my number and hand the phone back to her. We walk to the patio door.

"Later," Kiki says and heads down the hallway with Elvis following close behind.

I continue exploring. In the room directly across from the patio, through the half-opened door, I see an elderly couple, a middle-aged woman, and three teenage boys, all crying and consoling each other while a man of about forty lies in the bed, eyes shut, unconscious. Or maybe dead. Hard to tell. The older woman sees me looking in and gently closes the door. A skeleton of a man with a pointy head and sunken cheeks shuffles down the hall toward me. As he gets close, he gives off a sickening smell like a compost bucket that should have been emptied days ago. My head feels all floaty and what breakfast might be left in my stomach is threatening to make a reappearance.

I sprint for the door.

Chapter 11

Declan runs a scalpel down the white belly of a rat. Purplish tissue covers the guts and organs. He sprinkles the incision with white bleach powder, cuts the anklebone, and pulls back the fur. This is no longer a living thing—just organic matter.

After bolting from the hospice, I decided to bike the long way home to avoid any bridges. I rode Main to East 12th to Declan's house. No surprise that Izzy and Ty were already here, glued to a video game.

Declan's dark musty basement is our hangout. Cobwebs droop off old wooden beams and only two small windows let in natural light. Declan's parents must hear the loud music upstairs, but they never come down. When we get hungry, Declan goes upstairs and empties the fridge of delicious leftovers—paneer, spicy dahl, veggie samosas, homemade naan bread, and chai tea. If we're still hungry after we clean out the fridge, one of us heads to the corner store a few blocks away for Cheezies, BBQ chips, and Snickers bars—our snacks of choice.

I change the record on the turntable in the large wooden cabinet. We sometimes go hardcore retro and listen to Declan's great-aunt's ancient vinyl records of Elvis, Patsy Cline, Chuck Berry, and soundtracks from old 60s movies like *The Sound of Music, West Side Story,* and *My Fair Lady.* I replace Herb Alpert and the Tijuana Brass with Harry Belafonte, set the needle on the record—which makes a crackling sound—and pump up the volume.

"Everybody ready?" I ask.

All of us know the words to "Day O" by heart and sing as loud and obnoxiously as we can.

> *Day O, Da-a-ay O.*
> *Daylight come and me wan' go home.*
> *Day, me say day, me say day O ...*

When the song ends, my throat hurts from belting out

the words with Harry, but I feel a bit lighter somehow. I turn down the stereo.

Izzy and Ty battle it out on the video game. A ripped brown leather couch, the old family TV, and all the latest and greatest video games are the other reasons why Declan's basement is the hangout of choice. Ty keeps his thumbs wiggling on the game controller, doesn't take his eyes off the TV screen. There's a loud explosion. Izzy moans.

"Yes!" Ty pumps one arm in the air and quickly goes back to the game.

I watch as Declan pulls off the rat's skin and snips the front anklebone. He cuts around the skull and the mouth, then peels the pelt from the body and plops the hide into a fluid that smells like stiff booze. I wonder why I could have the stomach for dead rat, yet barf up my breakfast after biking across a bridge.

"Have to cure the hide before I mount it and breathe life back into this beautiful creature," Declan says.

"Why do you love taxidermy so much?" I ask.

Declan thinks for a moment. "Maybe because it combines life, death, art, and science."

"It's disrespectful to exploit animals, Declan," Izzy calls out.

"I don't exploit animals," Declan says. "Most people wear leather boots and buy their faceless, anonymous meat at the grocery store without a thought of where they came from. This craft is not about brutality, but capturing the beauty of living creatures."

"You have to admit, it's a bizarre pastime, D," I say.

"Maybe, but it wasn't just teenagers leaning to the dark side at the course I took. There was also a doctor, a lawyer, a computer programmer, and a stay-at-home mom. Taxidermy has become quite the hipster hobby."

Another explosion from the video game. "No! Not again!" Izzy yells.

Declan will stuff almost any dead animal he finds in a park or by the side of the road that doesn't look like a bloody pancake. I'm not sure he captures much beauty in the dead animals he stuffs, but his creations sure express his warped sense of humor. A stuffed raccoon paddles a small birch bark canoe; two crows sit at a table, wearing backwards baseball caps and playing Texas Hold'em;

a fluffy white cat with googly eyes and an evil grin rides a tiny skateboard with a skull painted on it. There's a hummingbird with iridescent green feathers, sitting on the table, that Declan's cat Matrix brought into the house. Declan has yet to breathe life back into this tiny beauty.

A wax museum image of Will flashes through my mind. Wearing his soccer uniform, muscular leg reaching for the ball. I suddenly feel claustrophobic—like I can't breathe.

"I need fresh air," I say, gathering my purse and jacket.

"What?" Ty looks up for the first time in about a half-hour. "You just got here. Wait till this game is over and I'll drive you."

"I'm going now."

"Just one more level." Ty focuses back on his video game. "You will be destroyed, once and for all, Izzy."

"I'm leaving," I say and head for the stairs.

"Geez. I'll quit the game, then," Ty says, pissed. He puts down the controller.

"Don't bother!" I snap.

Izzy and Declan share an awkward look. I run up the stairs and out the door.

In my bedroom, I import the photos from my phone onto my laptop. Title the album "Bridge." I scroll through the pictures to find the one of Will smiling. I click on Edit and try out a few different filters to brighten his image.

My phone rings. Ty. Decline the call. Text from Izzy: *U ok? Wanna talk?* Text from Ty: *Can I come over?* Another text: *Sorry if I pissed u off.*

I turn off my cellphone. Have a sharp ache in my stomach as I crop Will's photograph. I was there on the bridge. I was spying on him with my camera. A stranger. An intruder. I had no idea what he was going to do, and I feel sick about it.

When all the photos of Will are edited, I view them as a slow, excruciating slideshow. Then I click on each image like a stop-motion film. But the film stops with Will looking over the edge. In my mind, I conjure the white puffed-up shirt plummeting toward the water. My body begins to tremble from deep inside. I hold my hands together to try to stop them from shaking. I imagine I'm on the bridge. Climbing over the railing. Pushing off. Nothing to break my fall. I feel weightless, free.

I print off a few of the photos. There's a sharp knock at my door. I close my laptop and wait for the final photo to print before I open the door a crack. Dad's eyes look all squinty and stressed. Belle is in her room, wailing like a siren.

"Please help Belle find her red bow. It's probably somewhere in her room." Deep lines carve into his forehead.

"All that commotion for a stupid bow?" I say.

Dad shrugs. He's obviously exasperated.

"I'll be there in a minute." I close my door and breathe deeply several times to try to stop the trembling in my body.

Belle is curled up in bed on her very pink duvet in her very pink room. Her arm is over her face.

"What's got your panties in a knot, Belle?"

"M-m-y red bow's gone. My b-bow." Lots of snuffling and snorting. Belle wipes her snot all over the very pink flowers on her pillowcase.

"What's so special about the red bow, anyway?"

"It's so p-pretty, that's what. And it's red."

"When did you wear it last?"

"I dunno." She sniffs.

I ransack her drawers and rifle through all the junk in her closet. I reach under her bed and pull out a dusty pair of jeans, a hairbrush, and a sparkly silver Christmas ornament. I also find a whole pile of pamphlets and brochures. Belle is a brochure klepto. She collects them wherever she goes—grocery stores, banks, cafés, Mom's clinic, the community center. The brochure on top is for Langley House. The cover picture is a chubby man-boy with Down syndrome, pushing a teenage girl in a wheelchair. Both are smiling like they've heard the funniest joke ever. Under the photo it reads: *Life Skills for Community Living*.

"Is this where you went with Mom and Dad, Belle?" I hold up the brochure.

"That's mine!" Belle grabs the brochure, takes a long look at the cover, and then throws it on the floor. "I want my red bow, my red one." She puts the pillow over her head. I hear a muffled wail.

I peer under the bed again and find a silver bow.

"What about this one?"

One eye peeks out from under the pillow. "N-no, Claire, that's not red! It's not red." She sobs even harder. I lie down on the bed beside her and comb my fingers through her hair for a few minutes to calm her down. Then I pin the bow in her hair.

"Look in the mirror, Belle." She raises her head and grabs a hand mirror from her bedside table to look at the ridiculous bow sticking out of the top of her head.

"See? You look beautiful, Bella-Belle."

A smile creeps across her face. She does look beautiful, as if a flashlight shines out of her eyes. A wave of warmth drops over the two of us like a net. A peace I haven't felt in weeks.

"What about the secret, C-Claire? You promised to tell me the secret," Belle says.

"It's not a secret anymore, Belle." I secure the bow and look at her in the mirror.

The only sound at the dinner table is the clanking of utensils on plates. Dad is his normal talkative self (not), and Belle, silver bow sticking out of her head like an unruly twig, is tired after her over-the-top hissy fit. Mom is very quiet and mostly just shuffles the quinoa and veggies around her plate. The silence is disturbing. Belle reaches out and holds Mom's hand.

"What's wrong, Mommy? Why you so s-sad?"

"Kathryn?" Dad looks embarrassed.

"I'm sorry." Mom scrapes her chair, then pushes herself away from the table and high-tails it upstairs.

"Mommy, where you going?" Belle asks. "Mom-my!"

I've never seen my mother unravel like this before—it scares me. Dad follows her upstairs. Belle wants to join them but I hold her back.

As I load the last of the dinner dishes into the dishwasher, Dad comes into the kitchen and puts the kettle on. "What's going on?" I ask.

"It's Julius—he's dying." Dad gets out the teapot and some herbal tea.

Julius, well into his eighties, has been my mom's patient for about fifteen years. The first time I met Julius I was about eight. Mom and I ran into him shopping at the grocery store. You could tell he worshipped her as if she were some kind of healing goddess.

Apparently he loved to tell her doctor jokes, probably read them in *Reader's Digest*. I still remember the one he told me at the store. He used my name: Claire goes to see the doctor. She's got a pea in one nostril, a grape in the other, and a string bean stuck in her ear. Claire says to the doctor, "I don't feel well." The doctor replies, "The problem is clear to me. You're not eating right!" After Julius told the joke, he broke out into a loud belly laugh. Mom's smile was as big and bright as I'd ever seen it. Julius bent down and gently cupped my cheek in his hand and, when we were leaving the store, he bought me a lollipop. I could see why he was her favorite patient.

"How long does he have?" I ask.

"Weeks, maybe a month."

"That's so sad."

"D-Dad-dy, fill my bathtub. Now, please, now!" Belle's booming order bounces off the walls.

"Coming, Bella-Belle." Sometimes I think Belle could walk Dad around on a leash.

I bring the teapot and a mug into my parents' room.

Mom lies on top of the bed in the dimly lit room. I want to tell her I'm feeling sad, too, and that death really sucks. But I can't bring myself to. I put down the tea and lie down behind her. She takes my arm and wraps it tightly around her. I know I can't handle her sadness for very long. After a few minutes, I unwrap myself, pat her shoulder, and leave.

Alone in the studio. Dad's newest work-in-progress is different from his usual style. It has geometric patterns, circles, half circles, triangles, and squares—all melding into each other. Instead of his signature pulsating oranges, yellows, and violets, he's painted the shapes black, white, dark and gray. The painting energizes me—like when I listen to heavy metal music—but feels strangely comforting at the same time. I wonder if Dad's picking up on all the sadness I'm feeling. Or maybe he has grief of his own he can only express through his painting.

I tack up the smiling photo of Will I printed and put a brand new canvas on the easel in front of me. I start to sketch Will's face with a pencil, but it's coming out all wrong. I try again and again, but I can't get it right.

One thing that got me up every morning ... One thing that I was good at ... gave me hope for my future. When that was taken away, there wasn't much left to hang around for.

I push the canvas off the easel and throw the pencil across the studio. I feel like I'm slowly drowning. I struggle to hold my head above water, but it keeps slipping under. Constantly gasping for breath. What do I have left to hang around for? I stuff Will's photo back into my sketchbook and go to Dad's sacred corner of the studio. I plop down on the meditation cushion, hoping to find some of the peace and optimism he seems to have plenty of. I sit up straight, cross-legged like he does, rest my hands on my thighs, and focus my eyes on a red swirl on the area rug in front of me. I try to let my thoughts go, gently, like pushing bubbles with a feather ... Izzy's bright pink mini-skirt ... Belle's bow sticking out of her head ... Ty playing a video game ... holding my mom ... the rat's skin pulled from its body ...

the walking skeleton at the hospice ... Will's smiling face ...
me sitting in front of a thousand blank canvases.

Chapter 12

Kiki closes her eyes. Her mouth twitches as if she's straining soup through her teeth. She circles a deck of cards in the air and chants, "Ommapappabadadum, Ommapappabadadum, Ommapappabadadum." She opens one eye just a slit and looks at me being all nervous and jittery. And then she bursts out laughing.

"Ha, ha! Gotcha! Your face is so serious." Still chuckling, she hands me the deck of cards. "Shuffle these."

I'm at the cancer clinic with Kiki, and six other mostly bald people, who are lounging in Lazy-boy chairs and reading, sleeping, knitting, or doing crossword puzzles while they get their chemotherapy treatment. A long tube snakes from the needle in Kiki's hand up her arm to an IV-like bag hanging on a pole. I shuffle the cards on a table between us.

"Don't look so serious; this is supposed to be fun. To start, think of a question or some guidance you would like to have about your life," she says.

I slide small clumps of cards into other clumps. I have so many questions, I can't think of a specific one to ask. Is there life after death? Can Will communicate to me from the great beyond? Will I ever be inspired to paint again? I finish with the cards and hand them back to Kiki.

"Let's see what the tarot has to tell you," she says as she places six cards on the table. "Hmmm ..." Her eyebrows rise. Uh-oh.

My head spins as she talks about major and minor arcanas and cups and pentacles and wands and swords. It all sounds a bit *Lord of the Rings* to me. The first card is the Hierophant. It shows a picture of a religious, Pope-like figure wearing a crown and sitting on a throne.

Kiki reads from a tarot card book. "The Hierophant can represent confusion or a crisis of faith," she says. "He's also a teacher or wise man—someone you can turn to for help. See his raised hand? He's asking you to be still.

Listen to what's true in your heart."

"But how do I know what's really true?" I ask.

"Good question. I guess we're supposed to just intuitively know."

"Do you?"

She shrugs. "Haven't you ever known something to be true beyond a doubt, but you're not sure how you know it?" she says.

"Yeah, sometimes, I guess."

"This card also means you might meet someone who will help you figure it all out."

I thought Bernie would be my guide. He was there with me on the bridge, but all he did was pass me off to someone else.

Kiki picks up another card. "The Death card looks scary, but don't worry. It's nothing to be worried about."

Yeah, right. The card is a picture of a skeleton in black armor riding a white horse over what looks like a dead body. It creeps me right out. Am I grim reaper food or what?

"The Death card basically says that whatever is born eventually dies. When you get this card, you're supposed to ask yourself what part of you is changing or dying? Well, for me, that's a no-brainer. My body is being eaten up by a nasty disease called cancer. You?"

I don't feel comfortable enough with Kiki to spill my guts. I shrug. "There's change, all right."

"Who or what are you mourning?" Kiki looks at me like she wants me to answer the question. Out loud. My first reaction is to shut it down and not think about it. Not easy to do. Is it possible to mourn someone you didn't even know? Is that why I feel so crappy? Or is it watching the world slowly dying, like it has a sinister form of cancer? But the cancer is humans. Or am I mourning my art, the one thing that gives me hope in a hopeless world?

It's the Fool card that really gets me, though. This card shows a picture of a guy in tights who looks like a ballet dancer. He looks up into the sky, ready to take a flying leap off a cliff. He's happy. A little dog beside the fool looks like it's trying to warn him not to step over the edge. The sun shines from the top corner and the sky's a brilliant yellow.

"The fool is a fool when he is naïve and reckless," reads Kiki, "but this card also symbolizes faith. Fearlessly venturing over the precipice or the unknown. This card is telling you that sometimes we need to be willing to take a risk—to step into the abyss."

"You mean like *Indiana Jones and The Last Crusade*, when he's trying to save his father and he has to jump blindly into a deep, bottomless pit?" I ask.

"Exactly."

I've never been good at leaping into the unknown. I even hated being blindfolded for pin the tail on the donkey at birthday parties. I like my eyes wide open, thank you very much. But something about the fool card grips me right below my ribs. Is it because it reminds me of Will leaping off the bridge? Was it recklessness or some act of faith? In the tarot picture, the fool looks happy. Will was laughing while he talked on his cellphone to some guy named Jarret, seconds before he jumped.

"What do you need to explore, Claire? Where do you need to take a leap of faith?" Kiki looks at me intensely.

"Do you really believe in this tarot card stuff?"

Kiki holds up the fool card. "As the card says, you gotta have faith."

"Basically, I'm hooped," Kiki says, as I walk my bike with her to the bus stop. She seems exhausted after the treatment. "Doctors found a tumor on my ribs when I was eleven. After a few operations, chemo, and radiation, I did get better. For a while, anyway. And then this nasty thing called metastasis. The cancer spread to my lungs, which, strange as it sounds, was the best-case scenario. Better survival rate, apparently."

"Are you afraid ...?" I ask.

"More just pissed off I won't be able to live longer and experience more stuff. Ever heard of the Children's Wish Foundation?"

"Is that where sick kids get to go to Disneyland, swim with dolphins, or have lunch with a celebrity?"

"Yup. Well, my aunt wrote the foundation. When they contacted me, I told them my dying wish was to have sex, and could they make that happen, preferably with a hot guy."

"You didn't." I laugh harder than I have in weeks.

"I did. Just 'cause I'm dying, doesn't mean I don't get horny."

"You so rock!" I can't stop laughing.

"It didn't go over well. My mother and aunt were both angry as hell. They made me write a letter to apologize. I had to apologize for being honest."

We arrive at the bus stop.

"Thanks for hanging out with me. The cancer clinic isn't exactly fun times, I know. But my mom has to work and it's so effing boring by myself."

"Well, *you're* fun times."

"Ah, shucks. Thanks." Kiki hugs me. "When can we get together again? Promise I won't drag you to another chemo treatment."

"Soon," I say, putting on my bike helmet. "Maybe I'll see you at hospice. I still have to meet that Paul guy."

"Mr. Couvelier is a charming dude, but you haven't told me why you want to talk to him?"

Just then, Kiki's bus pulls up.

"Guess you'll have to spill it next time." Kiki gives me another quick hug and boards the bus. I watch as she sits in a seat by the window. Crosses her eyes, sticks out her tongue at me, and then waves.

I'm relieved. Not quite ready to talk to Kiki about the jumper. Maybe after I first talk to that charming dude, Mr. Couvelier.

Chapter 13

I look at my reflection in the bus window. Black lines of mascara circle my eyes and run down both cheeks, making me look like a morbid clown. One more reminder why I should never wear makeup, especially to a funeral. I clean myself up as best I can with a used Kleenex.

I stick my hand in my pocket. Yup, it's still there. Will's cellphone. I meant to hand it over to his family, I really did. But here it is, still in my pocket. I pull out my journal and my pen from my purse for the long ride home.

I went to your funeral. It took a few buses to get to East Van, but the last one stopped close to the church. I wore my black cords and my red satiny blouse, and did my hair in an up-do with my hairclip decorated with a fire opal from Mexico. Just to let you know, I don't dress up that often.

As I walked up the steps, I felt like you do when you dream you're naked in public. A few of your friends glanced over at me, wondering where I fit in. Everyone else seemed to know each other, talking softly, wiping tears, hugging. I walked through the large wooden doors and was handed a booklet with your picture on the front. Organ music played.

High up in the cathedral ceiling, sunlight passed through the stained-glass windows. One showed the image of Jesus hovering above an empty tomb. His halo looked like an astronaut's helmet. Two angels were looking up at him, ready to flap their wings and escort him to heaven. That image got me thinking ... didn't Jesus know the Romans were coming for him? I mean, he did have a direct line to the Big Guy. Could he have prevented his own death? And if so, by not escaping, did he commit suicide?

Your coffin was at the front of the church. That means they found your body (the newspaper was never clear on that). On top of the coffin was a big-ass photograph of you, book-ended by bouquets of white calla lilies. Off to one side, a display of soccer trophies, ribbons, and medals. Great smile in your photo, like you won the lottery or something. Like one of the photos I took of you on the bridge. Your cheeks carved into sharp angles at your chin like a square U, your forehead long, compared to the rest of your face. Your eyes looked a bit too big for your face but friendly. Don't get me wrong, you're hot—captain of the team and lead singer in the coolest band ever, wrapped in one beautiful package. This is going to sound warped, but I was kind of hoping your coffin would be open. I wanted to see you one last time, maybe even touch your hand or your cheek. Maybe seeing, feeling your dead body would somehow help me move on.

The last people to be seated must have been your family because they filed into the front pews with the Reserved sign. Including your parents and your sister. And Danielle. The photos on your cell definitely didn't do her justice. She's a beauty, that's for sure. Your family looked like the joy was sucked right out of them—like their hearts were broken forever.

Your friend Jarret said a few words. Because of my snooping, I know he's the one you were talking to on your cellphone right before you jumped. I wonder what he said to make you laugh. Anyway, he told the story of when you were both seven and smoked a whole pack of cigarettes behind Sam's Deli. He said your face turned green as grass. And when you were in Grade 8, you crazy-glued your teacher's shoes to the wall while she taught gym class.

Then your buddy David spoke. He said your nickname was Wonder Boy because you were the best right forward in soccer in the whole province. He finished by saying you were the best friend he will ever have— he choked on that last part. Waterworks all around. A few tears snuck down my cheeks.

After the funeral, the minister took your photo and the flowers off the coffin, and several buff guys I recognized from soccer photos hauled your coffin down the center aisle. Your family followed, and then everyone filed outside in front of the church. People rested their hands on your coffin as they walked by—a final goodbye before it was slid into a hearse.

I overheard someone say there would be no service at the crematorium. I was kind of hoping you'd be buried at the Mountain View Cemetery so I could visit you. Will you be bottled up and left on a shelf above the fireplace? Will your parents have joint custody? Or will you be scattered in a special place? I wonder where that would be. The soccer pitch?

I stood by myself in the corner of the church basement, eating a dill pickle and a tortilla roll filled with cream cheese and something green. Your friends were joking and laughing, which I thought was pretty rude. Videos were projected onto a screen: a martial arts competition when you were a kid, poking a fire while camping with your family. A recent video of you racing down the soccer field, finessing the ball away from opposing players, and scoring a goal. You had a big smile on your face while your teammates swarmed you. You walked up to the camera, stuck out your tongue, and gave it the finger.

A lot of people lined up to pay their respects to your family. I waited for my chance, even though I was light-headed and sweaty. But I needed to hand over your phone.

When the woman I presumed was your mother was finally by herself, I marched up to her. She reached out her hand and smiled sadly at me. I put down the tortilla, opened my mouth, but nothing came out, and my body started to shake uncontrollably. Then I did the thing that makes me hope I will never see any of these people ever again, so help me God. I threw my arms around her and started sobbing.

Your mom's voice is as smooth as creamy peanut butter. She kept saying, "He's in a better place now." Someone finally peeled me off her and I ran out of the church. After carrying on like that, I wouldn't have been caught dead (sorry) hanging around.

I get off at the bus stop near Kits Beach. After all that emotion at the funeral, I feel like all my skin has been shaved off with a razor. And I'm mortified I made such a fool of myself. I want to be alone but not alone at the same time. Wondering if I'll run into Ty, Izzy, or Declan. No one's here. I stick my face in the water fountain and let the icy water run down my cheeks until I can't feel anymore.

Soaked from the shoulders up, I continue down the path. A gray sky streaked with the odd black cloud has chased away any sunbathers. The cool breeze makes me shiver. I see Ellie sitting on the bench with her dead husband's name on it, overlooking English Bay. He died eight years ago at 97. Ellie keeps moving her head from side to side as if looking around a tree, but there isn't anything in front of her except English Bay. She breaks out into a big smile.

"Ellie?"

She looks up at me. "Oh, my, Claire, looks like someone got to you with a fire hose."

"What are you doing?"

"Just visiting with my little friend." Ellie moves her head again, then chuckles.

I look around but don't see anyone. "What little friend?"

"Rachel. She loves playing peek-a-boo."

I look, but there's no one there. "Are you feeling okay?"

"Doesn't know she's dead, poor dear." Ellie's always been a bit "out there" with her tea-leaf reading, but I wonder if she's had a stroke or is finally going bonkers. "Rachel is such a lonely little soul."

"Rachel's a ... ghost?" I start to get a little freaked out.

"I've told her to pass on, that her parents are waiting for her on the other side, but still she stays."

"You can talk to her?"

"Rachel and I ... communicate."

I sit down beside Ellie and look in the same direction. "How come I don't see her, then?"

She cups her leathery hand over mine. "Because you're looking with your eyes, my dear."

Chapter 14

"'I've come again to puncture the glory of the cosmos.' One of the best poets who ever walked the Earth—Rumi," Maggie says.

The Cosmic Cow is finally quiet enough for me to take apart and clean the espresso machine. Archie and Maggie play their poetry ping pong. Once a week they take turns choosing a theme, then let lines of poetry fly. It's Maggie's turn to choose the theme this week: everlasting.

"'We are such stuff as dreams are made on; and our little life is rounded with a sleep.' Prospero, *The Tempest*, Act 4, Scene 1," Archie hits back.

"Details only a Shakespeare scholar would ever remember," Maggie says as she pops out her fleshy boob and offers it to Bruin. Gag me. Gag Bruin, more like it. For the first time, I see him refuse the maternal fountain.

"'Going to heaven, how dim it sounds.' Emily Dickinson herself," Maggie says.

I say, "'Because I could not stop for Death—He kindly stopped for me.'"

"I didn't know you were a Dickinson fan, Claire," Maggie says.

"'I first surmised the Horses' Heads were toward Eternity.'" I thought I'd throw in the last line of the poem to impress them.

"Not bad," Archie says. "Tell me, Claire, what do you like about Dickinson?"

"She wrote poetry because she loved it," I say, "not because she wanted to make the big bucks or be famous. In her day, people thought her poems were weird, but that didn't stop her from writing. If she were alive today, she'd be like a rock star or something."

"What other poets do you like?" asks Maggie.

"I like Walt Whitman, Pablo Neruda, and spoken word poets like Sarah Kay and Shane Koyczan."

"Impressive," Archie says. "Have you studied poetry in school?"

"Yeah, from about fifth grade."

"And here I thought poetry would fade into oblivion with your generation," he says.

"Poetry is alive and well, Archie," Maggie says. "At university, my first and second year poetry classes sometimes even had waiting lists to get in."

"I'm heartened to hear that, my dear," Archie says.

Maggie and Archie smile at each other and carry on with their game. I sit down at the table by the window with Tessa and Celia.

Tessa, with a pile of bills in front of her, crunches numbers on the calculator, while Celia, Tessa's wife, works on her laptop.

"Hey, Buttercup," Tessa says to me.

"You're the only person I know who can be cheerful while paying bills," I say.

"It's just money, honey," Tessa says.

"Flows in ... flows out," Celia says, pushing her glasses up on her nose and typing away on her keyboard. She's probably writing up English lessons for the foreign students she teaches at Langara College.

"But sometimes I wish it would flow in just a little bit more," Tessa says.

"We're doing just fine, sweetheart," Celia says. She touches Tessa's arm lovingly, and gives her a look so hot it almost makes me blush. Tessa leans over and kisses Celia on the lips, then flips over another bill, and punches some numbers into the calculator. Ty told me he gets along well enough with Celia but really wishes his mom would have married Jeff, the boyfriend she had when he started fourth grade. He doesn't get that his mother is bisexual. In his mind, you're one way or the other, not both. Tessa once told me that, for her, it's always been the person she's fallen in love with, that gender has never mattered.

"Why don't you make yourself a Mango Wango wrap," Tessa says.

"Thanks, but I'm not hungry," I say.

"You're fading away, Claire," Celia says. "Pretty soon you're going to walk right out of your jeans."

I pull at my belt. My clothes are definitely roomier.

My shift is over. I'd planned to meet Ty at the Mountain View Cemetery, so I take the bus with Ellie for her weekly visit to her husband's grave. We get off the bus a few blocks away and stop at a corner store. Ellie takes me on a tour of the flowers stuffed in pails of water outside the store. It smells like a department store perfume aisle with all the competing fragrances.

"These are calla lilies, an elegant flower. Frank and I grew purple ones in our yard at our Kerrisdale house."

The calla lilies at Will's funeral flash through my mind.

"And these are gerberas. And roses, of course. Such a pretty pink color. And sunflowers. If you ask me, they are the happiest flower."

"Sure are." At least I'm pretty happy when I eat their seeds.

"Not many men care much about flowers, but my Frank loved yellow daisies." She takes a handful of daisies out of a pail and shakes off the water. "He even wanted to name our daughter Daisy. I told him that the one who carries the baby for nine months gets to choose the name, so I chose

Reta, after my aunt." She takes one last close look at the yellow daisies. "I'll go pay and be out in a jiff."

Ellie slips her hand around my arm as we walk through the cemetery. At this moment, I realize how much I love her and how sad I'll be when she dies. Why are gravestones and monuments mostly gray or black? So depressing. We come across a large sign on a stand that reads: *Light a candle, place a flower, speak the names of the dead.*

"Frank, my dearest," Ellie says with a sad smile.

Will, I say to myself.

We arrive at Frank's grave. At least it's made out of shiny brown marble. The engraving says: *In loving memory of a dear husband and father, Franklin Thomas Goodearl.* A quote at the bottom reads: *Death is not a foe, but an inevitable adventure.*

I wonder what kind of adventure Will might be on. Playing soccer in the clouds? Or is he like Rachel, the dead girl Ellie visits, who hasn't "crossed over"? That thought freaks me out.

"Someday soon, I'll be joining Frank on his adventure."

Ellie takes out the brown crispy petals from a small vase by the headstone. She pulls out a water bottle from her purse, fills the vase, and sticks in the daisies.

"Does Frank ever … show up here?"

"No, he likes to watch me while I'm working on my balcony planters. Still has the nerve to tell me how to prune my roses. Or he shows up in the kitchen first thing in the morning, waiting for me to make him his bacon and eggs, I guess."

"If Frank doesn't show up here, why come?"

"It's quiet and pretty. Besides, there are others for me to visit."

"Did you ever read Frank's tea leaves?"

"Oh, dear God, no. He thought I was a bit off in the head when I had the ladies 'round for readings. He would say it was all a bunch of bunk. That is, until I tracked down his mother's will."

"What happened?" I help her to her feet. She eases herself onto a bench by Frank's grave.

"Bessie, Frank's mother, asked me to read her tea leaves about a month before she died. I saw the shape of a cross in her cup and knew she didn't have much time left. Frank rolled his eyes clear up to heaven when I told him to make sure his mother had her affairs in order. Well, of course, she passed only a few weeks later, and not even a bloodhound would have been able to sniff out her will.

"A couple of days after she died, I woke up in the middle of the night—there was Bessie at the foot of our bed, with her son right beside me, out cold and snoring like a freight train. Bessie said, 'For heaven's sake, I told Frank years ago the will was in my gold brocade bag.' Well, when I told Frank that Bessie paid us a visit in the night and told me her will was in the brocade bag, he said I needed to get my head examined. So I said, suit yourself. But that didn't stop him from rummaging top to bottom through her house until he found the bag in the attic. And guess what? It had the will in it. That bag would have been given away to the Sally Ann with the rest of her things had she not woken me up to tell me."

"What did Frank say?"

"Not a thing. But the next time the ladies came over, I caught him listening by the door."

"Can you talk to any dead person?" I ask, wondering if

she could chat with Will for me.

"I don't like to be nosey. I usually just wait for them to come to me."

Even though the air is warm and still, I feel a breath of cold wind beside me. It gives me goose bumps, and the hairs on my arms stand on end.

Ellie's mouth slowly opens into a big smile. "That swoosh of air around you is Percy. He's standing right beside you."

I turn my head and see absolutely nothing. Now I'm totally creeped out.

I get up and say, "I'd better get going," but her attention is already focused on Percy. Some dead guy.

Chapter 15

Ty and I lie on the grass beside an ornate tombstone—a large angel about ten feet tall, bowing her head in prayer. The grass is scratchy on my bare legs and I feel cold when the sun hides behind a clump of puffy white clouds. The air between us feels prickly. I'm still mad at him for choosing to play a video game over spending time with me. He puts his leg against mine to see whose is longer. His, by about two inches.

"Hey, I see a dragon," he says.

"Where?"

"Right up there, see? The long nose, the puff of smoke, tail ..."

"A caterpillar, more like."

"Come on, it's a dragon," he says.

"No way."

"Can I have my way for a change?"

"Then just start, would you?" But I'm not really feeling like story time.

He sticks out his elbows and rests his head in his hands. I roll on my side and play with one of his long sun-bleached curls.

"There once was a seventeen-year-old girl named Muriel ..." he says.

"Muriel?"

"Her name's Venus, then."

"Venus? Was she named after the goddess, the tennis player, or the planet?"

"Would you just let me start the story?"

I yank on his hair, roll onto my back, and close my eyes.

"Venus lived all alone in a small cabin in a forest in Transylvania."

"Why did she live alone?" I interject, just to piss him off.

"Because her parents died of some bizarre fungal disease from tea they made from spruce needles. Venus had no other relatives around to take care of her, so she had made friends with all the animals in the forest, like deer, moose, birds, bears."

"Now you're getting all Snow White," I say.

"You're a pain in the ass. Would you just let me tell the story? Her human friend was Marley, an organic farmer who sold vegetables to people who lived in the forest. Your turn."

"Venus and Marley decided to make a huge pot of vegetarian chili and bake corn bread on a roaring fire just outside of Venus's cabin," I say.

"The deer, elk, squirrels, chipmunks, beavers, and humming birds all gathered round to partake in the magnificent feast," Ty said.

"After they ate, everyone got so chilled out, they lay down and fell asleep. An ember from the fire started to smolder. While they slept, Venus's cabin burned right to the ground."

"Venus wasn't homeless for long," Ty continues. "She found a hollow in a monster fir tree and set up a nice bachelor suite."

I jump in. "But soon after Venus hung the last pine-cone-framed photo of her parents, hurricane-force winds whipped through the area and decimated the forest."

Ty jumps in. "But the community rallied round and used the fallen timbers to rebuild—"

I interrupt. "—but the disaster was too much for Venus, so she and Marley together headed for the big city. Venus had never left the forest in her whole life, so—"

Ty interrupts. "So ... she was seriously freaked out by the crowds of people, skyscrapers, honking horns, and traffic jams. But Marley, being the good friend that he was, set her up in a nice two-bedroom apartment and paid her first and last month's rent. Venus got a job at Tim Horton's and became quite addicted to Boston cream donuts. She and Marley continued their friendship and often went to see Marvel movies together."

My turn. "One night at midnight, after her shift, Venus, high on sugar and caffeine, left Timmy Ho's. A gas-guzzling pig of an SUV with tinted windows careened around a corner. Shots were fired from the vehicle. Shots were returned from gang members in an alley close by. Venus got caught in the crossfire and was shot four times. Her last words were 'Boston cream, Boston cream ....' Venus died in the ambulance on the way to the hospital. The End."

"You can't do that." Ty says.

"Can't do what?"

"You can't kill her off. We made a deal—happy endings, right?"

"Well, not all endings are happy, are they?" I sit up. Cross my arms. My inner bitch is beginning to surface.

"Geez, Claire."

"What? I need to lighten up? Is that what you were going to say? That I'm still too moody?"

"I didn't say that. Trust me, I am trying to understand ..."

"Don't you think that maybe I have a good reason to be a bit depressed?"

"Yeah, of course. You saw a guy off himself. That was really messed up, but ..."

"But what? Just get over it?" I get to my feet. "Is that what you're thinking?" He just stares at the ground. I grab my handbag and quickly walk away.

"Can we just talk about this? Claire ..."

I race-walk through the tombstones and he doesn't even bother to follow me.

I'm cracked wide open. Raw. It feels like I'm being pulled into a dark hole that I can't climb out of. I'm desperate. Have to talk to someone.

I take the bus to St. Michael's and a nurse tells me Paul's in a meeting. I walk down the hall to the smoking patio and see Kiki through the window. Elvis wags his tail when I open the door.

"Well, look who's here," Kiki says, and flicks ashes from her cigarette into the ashtray.

"Hi." I sit down on the cold plastic chair.

"You look pretty rough. Something happen?"

I gesture at a package of cigarettes on the table. "Can I have one of those?"

"Sure." Kiki gives me a cigarette and strikes a match for me to light it. I suck as many carcinogens and other toxins into my lungs as I can and then immediately have a coughing fit. My throat burns and my eyes and nose won't stop watering. I wipe my face on my sleeve.

"Whoa, slow down there, girl. What's going on with you?"

"Had a fight with my boyfriend. We broke up." At least, I think we broke up. I look at the burning tip of my cigarette.

"That sucks."

"It's more than that. Way more." My voice sounds weak and jittery.

"Want to talk about it?"

I tell Kiki about the bridge, the jumper, the cop, my smothering parents—the Coles Notes version—but I get the point across that I'm messed up.

"Holy. That's some serious shit to sort out. But you've come to the right place. Paul's definitely your guy."

I butt out the cigarette. "Sorry," I say, holding up the cigarette. "I'm an idiot."

"Hey, no worries. I can still smoke the rest of it." Kiki takes what's left of the cigarette and puts it back into the pack.

Paul opens the patio door. Elvis wakes from his sleep and wags his tail.

"If it's not the man himself," Kiki says.

"I was wondering where the party was," he says.

Kiki smiles. "You were supposed to bring the six-pack."

"Damn!" He smacks his forehead with the palm of his hand. "Must have slipped my mind. By the way, Sunshine, at least you get to party. Time for your meds." He looks at me. "Have we met?"

Kiki jumps in before I have a chance. "This is my friend, Claire, and she wants to talk to you, so make time for her, okay?"

"Yes, Sergeant Major." Paul salutes Kiki, then shakes my hand.

Kiki stubs out her cigarette in the ashtray and walks to the patio door.

"We love it when Kiki's mom goes away," Paul says as he gives her a big hug. "We get her all to ourselves." He puts her in a headlock and gives her a noogie. She hugs him as if he's her dad or her uncle. Seeing how comfortable she is with Paul quiets the niggling anxious feeling I have about being here. Maybe he is someone I can talk to.

"Call me?" Kiki says to me as she leaves the patio with Elvis trailing close behind.

"Come on then, let's talk," Paul says.

We leave the hospice and walk down a street, to where, I'm not sure. For a chubby guy with such short legs, he can really move.

"Ewing Sarcoma," Paul says. "That's the aggressive bugger that's invaded Kiki."

Along the street are rundown houses with broken windows and boarded-up doors. On the front porch of one house, I see two sleeping bags, like giant cocoons, with heads sticking out.

"Is she going to die soon?" My words come out all choked up.

"Hard to say. She's a fighter, that's for sure. Digging those fingernails in and clinging with all her might. Never witnessed anyone hold on to life as relentlessly as Kiki."

"It's not fair—she's only about my age."

"Nope, it sure isn't fair. But it is what it is."

We walk toward a scruffy man with wild wiry hair sticking out all over the place, arguing loudly with himself.

"Hey, Larry, how's it going, buddy?" Paul asks. The stench coming from this man—a combination of piss and body odor—almost knocks me to the ground. Paul slips a five-dollar bill into Larry's hand. I get the feeling I'm not supposed to see the exchange of cash. But Larry just looks at the bill in his hand without even acknowledging the giver, stuffs it into his pocket, and continues the argument with the voices in his head.

Paul and I end up a few blocks from the hospice at an ice cream shop with a sign that says: *You Scream I Scream.* A bell dingles when the door opens. The place has four small tables with red and white checkered tablecloths and a few stools at the counter. On the wall are old black and white photographs of horse-drawn milk carts, hand-cranked ice cream makers, and glass milk bottles. The freezer at the front has a dozen tubs of ice cream and sorbets.

"What flavor would you like?" Paul asks.

"Strawberry."

"Sprinkles?"

"Sure."

"Grab us a table and I'll be right back with your strawberries and cream super-duper scoop in a waffle cone. You'll be so hooked after this."

"This stuff's like crack," he says when he brings the ice cream to the table. He licks his double chocolate fudge mocha cone and lets out a moan of ecstasy so loud the couple at the next table look over at us. "My doctor keeps telling me to stay away from it." He holds up his cone in one hand, puts his other on his bulging belly. "But we all have our addictions, right?"

"Right," I say weakly, trying to figure out what mine are. And then I think about how I cling so tightly to Will's cellphone, not wanting to give it up, even to the police. Is that an addiction? I lick the chocolate sprinkles off my strawberries and cream. The coolness feels good on my tongue and lips.

"So, Claire. I'm all ears."

"Well, actually, Bernie sent me. He thought I should talk to you." I sink my lips into the ice cream.

"Bernie?" He looks puzzled.

"I mean Bernard ... Bernard Oswald."

"Oh, Bernard." He laughs a little too loudly and again the neighbors at the next table look over. "You really call him Bernie to his face?"

"Well, no." Now I'm super embarrassed. It's sometimes hard to keep my inside voice inside.

"He's a good guy. He was instrumental in helping me get some Vancouver fat cats to lighten their wallets for our hospice renovation. How do you know Bernie?" he says, exaggerating the "Bernie."

"We were both on the Lions Gate Bridge. The day Will Szabo jumped. You probably heard about it in the news."

Paul is silent for a moment, taking it in. Not even licking his ice cream. "Bloody hell." He looks at me closely as if he's waiting for me to scream or burst into tears. After a few minutes, "Tell me about it."

"I was the last person to see Will alive. He looked right at me and said he was sorry. But everything happened so fast, it's a bit of a blur." I surprise myself, opening up to Paul like this. Maybe he's some kind of hypnotist and I'm under his spell. "I went to Mr. Oswald's office, hoping we could discuss it. I mean, we were both there on the bridge. But he wasn't interested in talking to me. All he said was Will's suicide was wasted potential—as if Will's life was like a science experiment that failed. That really pissed me off."

"Hmmm ... that would really piss me off, too." Paul bites off a big hunk of waffle cone and crunches it down.

My ice cream starts to melt so I lick it again.

"Witnessing someone take their own life must have

been pretty brutal," Paul says. "How've you been coping?"

I shrug. "Fine, I guess." Fine. There's that word again.

"You guess? So why are we talking?"

I hesitate, again wondering why I'm about to unload on a total stranger. "Not fine. Pretty screwed up, actually." I'm getting used to this quivery sound in my voice.

"What's happening with you?"

Words gush out of me. "I sleep too little or I sleep too much. I drag my ass around every day in a dark fog. My parents are worried about me; my friends think I'm psycho; and ..." I start to really choke up, "I can't do my art anymore. Every time I pick up a paintbrush or sketching pencil ..." Tears leak down my face faster than I can wipe them away with my shirt sleeve. I'm now blubbering, feeling over-the-top and conscious of the same people looking over at me this time. Paul hands me a napkin. I blow my nose. "Even when I doodled, it was like I was feeding a monster that's always hungry. Now I feel so empty."

"Sounds like art is your soul food," Paul says.

"I just want to get back in control." I let out a big breath. "Back to some kind of normal. I want my parents to stop worrying about me. I don't want to drag my friends down anymore, especially my boyfriend. And I want to be able to paint again." I blow my nose into a napkin.

Paul leans toward me and looks right into my eyes. "Well, Claire, to be honest with you, I think control and normal are overrated. Sometimes the best way to get to the other side is to go right through the pain, yelling, kicking, and screaming like a crazed fool. Believe me, I've been there."

"I just want to understand."

"Understand why a guy would want to kill himself? Wow, that's a pretty tall order for anybody." Paul sighs heavily, scarfs down the rest of his cone, wipes his face with a napkin. "Here's the thing. First of all, I guess you could say I'm more of a philosopher than a counselor. I do counsel people sometimes, and I think I'm pretty good at it, but I'm not a professional."

The fact that Paul isn't a professional makes it more than okay with me.

"And secondly, every time I think I have the answers, life slaps me upside the head to remind me what an insignificant little shit I am in the grand scheme of things.

So I've decided to be just an observer of sorts. But that doesn't mean I'm one to shirk the difficult questions. I'm booked for the next couple of days, but I'd be happy to meet up with you early next week and, together, maybe we can untangle the perplexing notions of life and death. But if I think you need more help than I can offer, I'll refer you to someone who has more tools in their toolbox than I do. You good with that?"

"You mean a shrink?

"Yup, that's what I mean."

I hesitate, nod, and take another soothing mouthful of ice cream.

Chapter 16

Will and I sit by a window at the Cosmic Cow. At the next table, a woman shovels Kalamata olives into her mouth with a soup ladle, which makes Tessa go ballistic because she never orders enough. I sketch Will with charcoal in thick black lines to exaggerate the sharp angles of his face, draw his eyes huge and his forehead extremely long. He takes a big drink of mocha that leaves a whipping-cream moustache. I sketch it in the portrait, so he puts another daub on his chin to make a goatee. We both laugh like it's the funniest thing in the world. We look out the window at an old woman who looks like a peasant in a long dress, apron, and a headscarf tied under her chin. She has a thick rope slung over her shoulder and hauls an enormous broken clock—springs and components sticking out everywhere like a metal Afro. I want Will to talk to me about his life, why he offed himself, what it's like on the "other side," but he says the time's not right. I ask him why and he doesn't say anything for a long time. "Because you're not ready to hear it," he finally says. And then he leans across the table and gives me a whipping cream kiss on the lips. I lick it off.

I wake up and dig out my journal.

In my dream you told me the time wasn't right to tell me about yourself and why you ended your life. You said I'm not ready to hear. I accept that. But I don't like to be kept in the dark about anything. I also like a challenge and I'm determined to figure you out. And hopefully save myself in the process.

After spilling my guts to Paul, it feels like that crushing weight is slowly being lifted off me.

I'm finally ready. I searched "411" online and found

twelve entries for "Szabo" in Vancouver. Will was obviously not concerned about online privacy and security because I was able to find out where he lived in less than three minutes. In an Instagram post, Will mentioned he lived right around the corner from Has Bean coffee shop, and Google maps helped me zero in on his address.

I take the bus to East Vancouver through streets with old apartment buildings and corner stores. I get off the bus and walk a few blocks to Will's house.

There are many renovated houses on the block between white boxy homes Dad calls "Vancouver specials." Will's is one of the spruced-up ones: a newly painted brown two-story with a tall peak. The trim around the windows and doors is a bright friendly yellow. Plant pots, teeming with orange and pink flowers, line the steps to the front door. The only thing that doesn't fit is the long grass choked with dandelions.

I slowly walk up the stairs and ring the doorbell. No answer. I knock a few times. Nothing. I walk to the backyard. The grass is overgrown here, too. Folded-up chairs and a patio umbrella lean against the house. A round table stands alone on the gray cement.

I can't very well leave the cellphone at the front of the house. There's no mailbox hanging by the door, only a skinny slot for letters. So I take a pen out of my purse and write a note at the top of a flyer collecting dust at the front door.

Hi, my name is Claire Winters. I have Will's cellphone. Call me on the cell to arrange a time when I can return it to you. Thank you.

As my note slides through the mail slot, I feel a strange mixture of relief and sadness. The phone won't be locked up in some evidence room at the police station. And I won't be hauled into an interview room or jail cell for questioning. I hope. The phone will be back with Will's family, where it belongs. But I wrestle with letting go of the only connection I have to him, suddenly feeling dizzy, like my head's floating away from my body. I flop down on the front step and imagine Will beside me, his arm around my shoulder, holding me close.

I make my way back to the bus stop down a different street. A few blocks from Will's house, I come to a huge field of green grass circled by a running track. A group of guys race down the final stretch of the field. One in black shorts and a white singlet totally blows off the others and beats them by about five seconds. He pumps his arms in the air when he crosses a white line. The rest bend over to catch their breath and then playfully punch the speed demon.

I walk through the field. The guys pair off and start passing soccer balls. They use some pretty fancy footwork to keep the ball away from each other. When I walk closer, I wonder if they were at Will's funeral, but I don't recognize any of them. I sit on the bleachers and watch the practice until it finishes.

When it's over, I walk up to three guys sitting on a bench and packing up. One looks up at me. Sweat glues his wavy brown hair to his head. "Hey."

"Hey," I say back, feeling squirmy, not exactly comfortable to be putting myself out there with these older guys.

"What's up?" he asks.

"Do you—I mean—did you know Will Szabo?"

The guys look at each other. "Yeah. Why?"

"I ... um ... what can you tell me about him?"

"What do you want to know?" says a guy with a chipped front tooth and a scar that runs diagonally down his left cheek.

"Like ... why Will would want to kill himself?" I feel like bolting as soon as the words sprint out of my mouth.

"Jesus," says the chipped-tooth guy. He's pissed at me. Stuffs a sweatshirt into his bag.

"Why would we want to talk to you about Will?" says the third guy, with purple-black skin and black hair so shiny it looks shellacked.

"Because I was there. When Will jumped off the bridge."

The three of them blurt out a chorus of "What the ...?" "Holy shit." "Bloody hell." They look at me differently. Almost sympathetically.

"We weren't exactly friends," says the brown-haired guy as he towels off his sweaty head and face. "None of us knew him that well. Will mostly kept to himself."

"He only played with our team for a few months and then tried out for the Whitecaps," says the black-haired guy.

"Whitecaps?" I ask.

"Vancouver's professional soccer team," the guy with brown hair says.

"Did he make the team?"

"After he left, he wasn't in touch much with anybody on this team. Just kind of disappeared from our soccer scene." Brown-haired guy peels off his socks. I can smell his stinky feet from where I'm standing.

"So you don't have any idea why he'd kill himself?"

The guys shrug, look uncomfortable.

"Look," says the black-haired guy, "maybe his girlfriend screwed around on him. Maybe he had credit card debt. Who the hell knows? Whatever it was, he wouldn't have confided in any of us." The other guys nod.

"Thanks, anyway." I start across the field.

"Hey," the brown-haired guy calls out.

I turn around.

"There's a party at Jericho Beach this Saturday night. You should come."

I wave and keep walking.

On the bus ride home, I replay Danielle's voicemail message on Will's cell: "Hi, it's me. I've been waiting for you. Did you forget?" Big sigh. "Well ... I guess if I don't hear from you, I'll just cab it home ... What's wrong? I'm so worried about you." Long pause. "You know I love you, right? Call me. I don't care how late it is."

I punch in a number.

"Yo, who's calling?" Ty says. "Hell-ooo, who's there?"

I end the call and say out loud, "You know I love you, right?" But it feels like I'm telling a lie.

An old Asian man in the seat in front turns around and glances at me. I space out for I don't know how long, then dial another number from my cellphone.

"Hello," Danielle's voice sounds sleepy, as if she just woke up.

"Hi, my name is Claire Winters."

"Yeah. And you are ...?"

"I, um ... I ... I ... was on the Lions Gate ... when Will jumped." I sound like a vinyl record skipping.

The old man turns around again and just stares at me. I cup my hand over the phone and turn my head to face the bus window.

"Is this a sick joke?" She sounds irritated.

"No, really. I was there."

A long silence. "You saw him jump?" She definitely

doesn't believe me.

"Yeah."

"You actually saw him climb over the railing and jump off the bridge into the water?"

"Yeah."

"Oh, my God." She now sounds emotional. I hear sniffling. "How did you get my number?"

What do I say? What do I say? "Found it on Facebook." I smack my head with the palm of my hand. What an idiot. Nobody uses Facebook anymore.

"You creeped me on Facebook?" Blows her nose.

"Yeah, sorry about that. Guess I haven't been thinking straight."

Silence.

The old man's forehead crinkles and he looks at me like I'm a certifiable lunatic.

"Can we meet? For a coffee or something?" I ask.

She makes a sound like air deflating from a balloon. "I'm trying to put things behind me right now. It's been a living nightmare."

If she witnessed Ty jump off a bridge, would I want to

talk to her? Probably not.

"It's been a nightmare for me, too," I tell her. "Please, I really need to talk to someone who knew him well."

When I get home, it feels like a tornado's blowing through the house. Dad, whose only speeds are slow and slower, is running around like he's being chased by a bear, collecting Belle's clothes from the laundry room and her DVDs from the TV room. Mom is rifling through the closet and packing Belle's sweaters and jackets into a suitcase.

"Where's the fire, for crying out loud?" I say. "Could everyone just slow down. You're hurting my brain." I open the fridge and take out a carton of blueberry yogurt.

"Trying to get out of here before the traffic gets too congested," Mom says.

"Where's Belle going?"

Mom puts Belle's suitcase down and her eyes dart to my father, then back at me. Dad pulls his ear in his I-don't-really-want-to-talk-about-it way.

"Belle's going to stay in Langley tonight, at the group home," Dad finally says. "There's a party and a dance at the community hall she wants to go to."

"What do you mean 'group home?'" I take a mouthful of yogurt.

Dad volleys this one to Mom. She hands me a brochure—the same one I saw in Belle's room. "Check it out online. It's a group home for young adults."

"A room's become available," Dad says. "Belle seems happy about giving it a try. She'll stay over for a few nights at a time and see how she likes it."

"You talked about a new program. You didn't say anything about Belle moving out of our house."

"We first wanted to see if Belle liked the staff and the other residents," Dad says.

"This is so typical." My voice is getting louder. "I'm always left out of every decision made in this family."

"The group home is in Langley, Claire, not the other end of the country," Mom says.

Rage builds. My face feels like it's on fire. "I can't believe you're sending Belle away."

"She can come home on weekends or holidays. Whenever she wants," Mom says. "They have programs in place that will give her far more opportunity to learn independent life skills, work skills ..."

"That's bullshit! What kind of parents are you? Your kid has Down syndrome, so you ship her off to let someone else look after her?" Now I'm yelling.

"It's all speculative at this point," Dad says. "We'll see how Belle likes living there first. No decision will be made until she's sure it's right for her."

"Dad, you of all people know how impressionable Belle is. Even if she didn't like the place, she wouldn't tell you. She'd do anything to please you."

"Your mom and I haven't made this decision lightly, Claire. We've researched, talked to people—professionals, other parents, workers in the group home. We came to the conclusion this is what's best for Belle. She's nineteen years old and should have the opportunity to live as normal a life as possible with people her own age."

"She's not normal, Dad. She'll never be normal. When are you going to accept that?"

Belle stomps into the kitchen, looking all Club Monaco in new jeans and a funky blouse. "S-s-s-stop yelling. J-just stop now!"

I throw my container of yogurt at the wall and storm out of the kitchen, run upstairs, and slam the bathroom door as loud as I can. Sobs convulse in my body and then explode.

"C-C-Claire. Why you c-crying? Why you so sad, Claire?" Belle says softly outside the door.

I turn on the shower to drown her out, sit down with my clothes on, letting the hot water pour over me. I hug my knees and try to rock the pain away.

Chapter 17

The espresso machine hums and hisses. Hard to whip up "Udderly Delectable lattes" and "Moo-cachinos" all day when I feel kick-boxed right below my ribs. I move like a robot stuck in super-slow speed. And although I can see the bright sun through the windows, it's as if I'm wearing dark sunglasses. Belle let loose on the world? Yeah, right. She can barely dress herself, let alone work at some job. My parents tried to smooth things over this morning before I left for work. But I was too furious to hear them out. Can't help but think they're big-time shirkers.

Izzy's whirlwind energy and shocking yellow and lime-green tie-dyed T-shirt jar me more than ever today. Her faster-than-the-speed-of-light chatter makes my head spin. Declan nicknamed Izzy "Babble-On." So appropriate.

I finish making one espresso drink and start the machine up for another.

"This guy I met at Jasmin's party was so hot, Claire. His name's Chris and he has a body like you wouldn't believe— tall with bulging muscles, just like Popeye. I don't think you've met Chris or you would have so dumped Ty on the spot and had a go with him. Well, he told me he liked my hair. I mean, really? Are you kidding me? My hair looks like someone held me by my feet and dipped my head in white paint."

"Izzy, please stop. You're hurting my head."

"Oh, yeah, sorry. Just that we don't talk much anymore." Izzy usually takes everything in stride, but I know I hurt her feelings.

"Izzy ..." I want to apologize, but she turns and storms into the kitchen.

"How you feelin', darlin'? You look tired today." Tessa comes up behind the counter and fills the cooler with fresh wraps.

"Yeah, I am tired. It's nothing," I say.

"When I'm finished with this, I'm going to make you my masterpiece creamy mocha shake with a dollop of my secret ingredient—almond butter. Cures everything."

"You don't have to do that, Tessa."

"I want to. Because I love you." She pulls me close, gives me a long hug, kisses my forehead, scoops up her tray, and hurries off to a table of customers. I wish I could stay in her arms forever. Love comes so easily to her, oozes out of every pore. Someone posted an article on Twitter that said scientists discovered a genetic mutation that may explain sociopathic behavior. Why not study Tessa? Look for the love gene and clone her many, many times over.

I'm working the regulars' table and bring Archie two shots of espresso. Bruin is sleeping soundly in Maggie's arms. Maggie's literary theme for the day is "fear."

"'Would the world ever have been made if its maker had been afraid of making trouble? Making life means making trouble.' George Bernard Shaw, *Pygmalion*," says Maggie. "Your turn."

Archie responds, "'Of all base passions fear is most accurs'd,' from *Henry VI,* Part One."

"My day wouldn't be complete without hearing you recite Shakespeare," Maggie chuckles, as she strokes Bruin's hair.

"I will mold you into a Shakespeare scholar one day, Maggie. I'm sure of that," Archie says. "Here's another from *Measure to Measure*: 'Virtue is bold, and goodness never fearful.'"

Tessa brings me her special smoothie and puts in her two cents' worth. "'If you have fear of some pain or suffering, you should examine whether there is anything you can do about it. If you can, there is no need to worry about it; if you cannot do anything, then there is also no need to worry.' The Dalai Lama himself." She namastes her hands together and bows to us.

"How about you, Claire? Do you want to recite a famous literary quote about 'fear'?" Archie asks.

"From *Little Women*: 'I'm not afraid of storms, for I'm learning how to sail my ship.'"

"That's lovely, honey," Tessa says.

I don't tell this to many people, but *Little Women* is one of my all-time favorite books. Jo is so kick-ass, and she follows her heart. I've read *Little Women* several times and I still cry when I come to the chapter where Beth dies. Declan, who's into Kurt Vonnegut, George Orwell, and Hunter S. Thompson, would laugh his ass off if he knew *Little Women* was my novel of choice. So I tell him it's *Fear and Loathing in Las Vegas.* He approves.

Bruin lets out a yowl just as Ty and Declan walk in. Ty goes behind the counter and grabs two wraps and takes them to the table where Declan is sitting.

Declan salutes me and Ty waves, but I just fold my arms and glare at Ty. After our fight at the cemetery, I can't seem to shake my anger toward him. He holds his hands up, like: *What the hell?* He keeps looking over at me while he and Declan dig into their food like they haven't eaten in days. Tessa, like Jesus, feeds the masses. Except rather than loaves and fishes, she feeds them with paninis, wraps, and smoothies. Izzy sits at the guys' table and the laughing begins. Declan gestures for me to join them but I can't face their joking. And I'm sure Ty and Izzy would rather I stay far, far away. Instead, I take a pot of tea to Ellie. Being with her is like sitting in a field of wildflowers on a warm summer day—calm and peaceful. She looks like royalty wearing a pastel green skirt with matching jacket and a string of pearls. I'm pretty sure her trademark orange lipstick glows in the dark.

She takes the teacup off the tray. "You must have been reading my mind, dear."

"No, mind reading's your thing, Ellie." I slump on a chair across from her, plunk my elbows on the table, hold up my head with my hands. It feels heavy, like one of those large black medicine balls we have to pass around in gym class.

"Ellie, could you contact someone for me? You know, from the other side?" Not that I entirely believe in her ability to communicate with dead people, but whatever she says to me always feels soothing.

"Let me tell you this, my girl. You don't need someone nattering at you from the other side, as you call it. Sometimes all they want to talk about is rubbish, anyway."

Declan comes to our table.

"You're looking especially stunning today, Ellie," he says. "That color really suits you."

"You are a dear boy, flattering an old woman," she says with a chuckle. Her cheeks turn pink.

"Claire, we're heading to the beach," Declan says. "Let's go."

"Can't. I have to bus with Belle to jazzercise or cross-fit, or whatever it is she's into now." I'm lying.

"Haven't seen much of you lately," he says. "Did you meet a new man or something? You can tell me. I won't spill it to Ty."

"Stuff's come up, that's all."

"Until we meet again," he says and makes his way to the door.

Izzy hurries a last load of dirty plates to the kitchen and joins the guys at the door. She looks over, gestures for me to come. I shake my head. She doesn't look happy with me as she follows Declan out. Ty gives me a sad smile and leaves.

"We had our problems, that's for sure." Danielle takes a sip of the chai latte I made her after the CC crowd died down. Her long blonde hair is tied in a messy knot on the top of her head. Even wearing sweat pants, a T-shirt with a faded Guess logo, and no makeup, she's still gorgeous. "Will was jealous as hell." Her forehead crinkles in a painful expression. "In the last months before he died, he started picking fights with any guy he thought was hitting on me. He beat up this guy outside a bar downtown. The guy looked at me—that was all. But it sent Will into this ridiculous rage."

"Was he always like that?"

"That's the thing. He was always jealous, but I was the only one who ever heard about it. He would never confront anyone, let alone punch them out."

She slowly twirls her latte mug on the table, gives me a look like she's told me too much.

"What do you think was going on for Will? You know, before he ..." I say.

She shrugs. "Things started to change after he banged up his knee. He needed surgery but it wasn't so bad. Doctors said that with physio, he'd make a full recovery. He did recover, but he still felt second-rate, like he would never play his best soccer ever again. Just a few months ago, he was asked to try out for an elite team. I thought—this is it, this will make him so happy. But it didn't."

"It doesn't seem like enough of a reason. You know, the

knee thing," I say, not sure Danielle is telling me everything.

"I didn't break Will's heart or anything, if that's what you're thinking."

"I wasn't thinking anything." Not true. I did wonder if she'd dumped him.

"You didn't know Will. He was obsessed. Soccer was his life. His everything. Soccer was way further up his life ladder than I was. When he didn't meet his own unrealistic expectations, he just seemed to get more and more depressed."

Painting is my everything. Now that my creative inspiration is in the toilet, I'm getting more and more depressed. Before this moment, I didn't realize how similar Will and I are.

"Was he ever depressed before his injury?" I ask.

"That's the thing. He was always so much fun and so upbeat. Almost too upbeat. Sometimes it felt fake. I mean, nobody can be that happy all the time. But after the surgery, he was in a big funk and all he did was mope around. And then the shit really hit the fan when he didn't get the scholarship he was counting on. When I tried to talk to him about his being so depressed, he told me I was imagining things." She wipes a tear rolling down her cheek.

One thing that I was good at ... was taken away ... there wasn't much left to hang around for.

I come home to a gloomy dinner. My parents and I barely exchange more than twenty words the whole meal. Mom is quiet, having just seen Julius, and Dad is the usual chatterbox. And Belle's not around to turn up the volume and take up space and airtime.

After dinner, I go into my room. The brochure for Belle's group home is on my bedside table. Pictures of parties, picnics, and camping trips. This is Belle's life, her future—not some summer camp. I punch in the number on the front cover.

"Hello," a woman's voice answers.

"Could I please speak with Belle Winters?"

"She's just finishing up loading the dishwasher ... let me get her."

Belle loading a dishwasher? I hear laughing in the background, the clinking of plates and cutlery.

"This is B-Belle."

"Hey, Belle."

"Claire, I cooked macaroni and ch-cheese for dinner. I did. Maya showed me how. And we got strawberries and fuzzy cream, too. We did."

"Wow, how come you never cook for me?" I ask. Belle lets out one of her from-the-boots belly laughs.

"Tomorrow it's chicken. I'm cooking ch-chicken with my friend Sam. You eat chicken, Claire?"

"You live with a boy named Sam?"

"Sam's not a boy, you silly." Another huge belly laugh. "S-s-am's a girl."

"I miss you, Belle."

"Why you sad, Claire? You're s-so sad."

"I love you, Bella-Belle." I end the call.

I pull on my headphones and listen to some relaxation music Tessa loaded on my cellphone. Soft, dreamy music with acoustic guitar accompanying the sounds of gentle waterfalls and chirping birds. I fall fast asleep and wake up in a sweat from a dream where I was pinned against a wall by a boulder crushing my bones.

Out my bedroom window, I see the light on in my dad's studio.

He's painting a series for a bank in downtown Vancouver. The canvas he's working on now is a spiral with muted colors at the wide end, more vibrant colors funneling in the center. It seems a bit backwards to me, but Dad somehow makes it work.

"Haven't had the pleasure of your company in here for a long time." He dips his brush and mixes Mars Black with Alizarin Purple.

I look around at my unfinished portraits for the Downtown Eastside silent auction. I feel overwhelmed, like a total failure.

"Pull up an easel and see what happens."

I watch his movement as he paints. Who needs the gym when you can break into a sweat brushing paint in large sweeping strokes from one side of an enormous canvas to the other?

"Dad, have you ever tried to paint, but all the inspiration

was sucked right out of you?"

"Yup. Comes with the territory."

"How did you get it back?"

"A looming deadline and a paycheck were usually my best motivators. Go easy on yourself. You've been through a lot. Maybe you just need a break for a while, to fill the well."

He loves quiet when he paints, but I need a jolt of audio stimulation to get my creativity flowing. Like Imagine Dragons or the Arctic Monkeys blasting out of the speakers.

"Dad?" I hold his iPod.

"Sure, go for it."

I search through his music and find an album that's kind of like a top twenty hits album of chanting Buddhist monks. Not exactly alternative rock, but it'll do.

I turn up the volume on the speaker. Great acoustics in the studio. Too bad Dad never lets me have a party in here.

Om Mani Padme Hum ... *Om Mani Padme Hum* ... It sounds like an army of monks chanting a simple melody. Other than their voices, the only instrument is a small bell that dings after every verse. Definitely not for metalheads.

"What do the words mean?" I ask.

"*Om Mani Padme Hum* is like a mantra. Chanting the words is meant to invoke compassion."

When your father's a Buddhist, compassion is a word you definitely want to look up in the dictionary, for blackmail if nothing else.

com·pas·sion/ kəm'paSHən/ Noun: sympathetic concern for the suffering of others.

Dad doesn't force his Buddhism down anyone's throat, but he does throw the compassion word around quite often as something for everyone in the world to strive for. He attends retreats where a whole bunch of Buddhists gather to discuss and meditate on sending compassion out into the world. Nothing wrong with that.

While the music plays, I close my eyes and imagine a sea of saffron-robed monks in a Tibetan monastery at the top of a mountain. Each monk sits in front of a candle, chanting. A calm feeling comes in a wave from the top of my head right down to my toes. After several minutes, I open my eyes.

"Dad, do you really think sending Belle off to live in a

group home is a compassionate thing to do?" I ask, not in a pissy way, for a change.

In his thoughtful way, Dad waits a long time before he answers. "I think the group home offers Belle a step toward independence that she deserves. Granted, she'll probably never be able to live on her own without some level of supervision, but this move gives her a chance to live an adult life—or at least a reasonable facsimile. This program in Langley has so many more options for Belle. So, yes, I feel we're doing the compassionate thing by allowing her to live her life to the fullest."

I'm still not convinced. Dad goes back to his painting, but I bypass my easel and pick up my sketchbook. Out falls the printed photos of Will I hid in there. I scramble to pick them up and shove them back between the pages before Dad sees. I turn the pages of the sketchbook: a grainy tree stump I sketched on the beach; Izzy laughing; a zombie with blood oozing out its mouth; a series of different-shaped noses; one big eye; and a guy and a girl kissing. The last page is the rough sketch of Will I started. Exaggerated square jaw and wide eyes but he's just a shell. And there's nothing I can do to bring him back to life.

Om Mani Padme Hum.

Chapter 18

I'm getting ready for bed when Will's cellphone rings. I have to hunt around where I hid it, in my bedside table drawer. Call display says *Lauren*. Will's sister.

"Hello," I say.

"Is this Claire Winters?" If you could feel Lauren's voice, it would be as soft as pussy willows.

"Yup, that's me."

"I'm Lauren Szabo, Will's sister."

"Yeah, hi. I have Will's cell, but I guess you knew that already." How can I waste precious phone charge being so lame?

"I got your note. Where did you find his phone?"

I shiver. "I was ... I was there ... when he ..."

Silence for a few long moments.

"You were on the Lions Gate?"

"Look, the phone's gonna run out of juice any minute." It actually still has about thirty percent charge, but I need to explain myself in person. "Can I just bring it to you tomorrow? Early afternoon work for you?"

"I'll be home," she says.

It's finally going to happen. I'm going to return Will's cellphone to his family. I hold it in my hand for several minutes. Like the true psycho I am, I can't totally let go. I turn to the back pages of my journal and write down every text, voicemail, and Instagram message in Will's phone. And, of course, I write out the suicide note. All that transcribing takes me over an hour.

Text on my phone. Ty: *Can we at least talk?* My cellphone rings. Ty. I let it go to voicemail. He phones again. No voicemail. I decide I'd rather chat with a dead guy, instead.

No wonder you fell for Danielle—she's beautiful. Disturbing what she said about you, though. How you changed from being the fun-loving guy to someone who sank into a depression and didn't come out. It scares me how much I can relate to you. I know what frustration and loss can do to a person. And I know how frustration and loss could make somebody want to call it quits and end their life. I ask myself almost every day if I could be pushed this far.

I flop on my bed, cover myself in the duvet, and cradle Will's cellphone on my neck. I imagine him crawling under the covers with me, kissing down my neck while he runs his hands all over my body.

I walk down the sidewalk, stand at the bottom of the steps. I don't want to give Will's cellphone back. Should I bolt? I want to hoard every text, photo, video, and Instagram message. Will his family blame me for not stopping him from jumping? They're surely going to wonder why I kept the phone so long. Nothing I can tell them will make any sense.

Lauren opens the front door. I recognize her from the funeral. She's about my age, petite, dressed in denim cut-offs. Her teal-colored spaghetti-strapped top with an enormous-

eyed anime character on the front reads: "Cuteness kills."
She peers down the steps at me. "You Claire?"

I nod.

"Come on in."

When I climb the stairs, I get a closer look at her.
She and Will don't look much alike, except maybe for
the shape of their faces. Her eyes, the color of the dark
hardwood floors in my house, are on the other end of the
color spectrum from Will's blue. She has an almost angelic
face—makeup-free except for an attempt to cover up a few
zits on her chin. Her thick black eyelashes definitely don't
need any mascara.

She leads me into the living room. It smells like a
combination of rosewater and cleaning detergent. There
are two formal-looking high-back chairs and a sofa with
gray velvety fabric, a needlepoint pillow on one of the
chairs of a robin in its nest, protecting its eggs. Over the
fireplace mantel is an ornate cross. Jesus isn't on the
cross, bleeding all over the place, but he does hang on the
wall in a cheesy paint-by-number. A blond and blue-eyed
Jesus (hello, Jesus was Middle-Eastern), stands with his

arms wide open on a grassy knoll, welcoming a group of children of all skin colors dressed in traditional costumes, like saris, ponchos, and grass skirts, while baby lambs and goats frolic in the background. Vases full of mostly white flowers, the petals turning brown, dot the room.

Will's mom comes into the living room, takes my hand in both of hers, and holds it for a long moment, like she did at the funeral.

"You must be Claire. I'm Patricia." She smiles warmly and looks intently into my eyes, which makes me squirm. I remember her stunning blue eyes from the funeral—obviously where Will got his eye color. She's short with a roundish middle, her hair brown with sparkling streaks of gray. She wears a navy below-the-knee skirt and a floral blouse. A cross hangs from a gold chain around her neck. "Thanks for coming," she says.

I stick my hand in my pocket and feel the phone. I pull it out, rub the smooth screen with my thumb one last time and hand it to Will's mom. She hesitates, then takes the phone. Studies it as if she's never seen a cellphone in her life, turns it around, looks at it from all angles. I'm worried she'll look through those disturbing photos of Will while I'm here. Lauren's cellphone bloops a text and she leaves the room, thumbing a response.

"I've got the kettle on," Patricia says. "Be back in a minute." She puts Will's phone down on the coffee table and goes into the kitchen. I have an overwhelming urge to grab it and run, but I snoop instead. I walk down a narrow hallway to find a super-sized photo of Will, about five years out of date, hanging on the wall behind a table filled with medals and trophies for soccer, hockey, and swimming. There's even a stack of Will's report cards. The ones from elementary school have so many gold stars pasted on them, there's barely enough room for the teachers' gushing words: *Star pupil ... Highest mark ... Top of the class.*

On the wall opposite the photo, a white karate jacket is tacked up along with a fan of cloth belts: white, yellow, orange, and green.

Lauren appears beside me. "He started karate when he was about five or six. Then he fell head over heels for soccer and never went back to martial arts. Even though his sensei said he would have gone far, of course." She says the "of course" with a sarcastic tone.

She picks up a small photo from the trophy table. Will, wearing his soccer jersey and a triumphant grin, sweaty hair stuck to his head, with his arm draped over Lauren's shoulder. So far, it's the only picture of her I've seen in the house. "When God doled out brains and brawn, Will got the lion's share in this family. I got the measly leftovers."

"Yeah, God can be unfair like that," I say, thinking of my own family. Seems like in the Szabo family, lopsidedness doesn't have much to do with Will's brains and brawn. After seeing this over-the-top shrine with barely a trace of Lauren anywhere else in the house, I wonder if it has more to do with Patricia favoring her son over her daughter.

"Tea's on," Patricia calls out. I follow Lauren back into the living room. Will's mom carries in a tray with a teapot, cups, and a plate of homemade cookies.

Lauren flops down on the couch and picks up Will's cellphone. She turns it on and is about to explore. "Not now, Lauren," Patricia says, putting her hand on Lauren's knee.

I'm so relieved when Lauren puts down the phone. I don't want to be around when they find the photos of Will or the suicide note. Patricia sits beside Lauren and pours the tea. I sit on the edge of the chair, not wanting to disturb the mother robin and her nest. Patricia hands me a cup of tea with tea leaves floating on the top and passes the plate of cookies. We sip and munch without saying a word for about thirty seconds. It feels like an eternity.

"Were you a friend of Will's?" Patricia says. "You look familiar."

"No, not a friend," I say, hoping like hell she doesn't remember the last time we met.

"Remember, Mom. Claire was there, when Will ..." Lauren says.

"Oh, yes, of course. I'm so sorry for that. I hope you haven't been troubled."

"I'm fine, thank you." Just fine. I take a bite of a chocolate chip cookie. I have this morbid curiosity to see Will's room and then scram. But how do I ask? There's another pause.

Lauren asks how I got Will's cellphone. I so wish I could just melt into a puddle on the carpet. I clear my throat. "He gave it to me."

"What?" Lauren says. "He just handed it to you before

he ..."

I nod and stare at the leaves floating in my tea.

"That's just sick." Lauren shakes her head, folds her arms.

More silence. Patricia looks either stunned or hurt. Maybe both.

"Did you snoop?" Lauren asks.

"Pardon?"

"Did you snoop through Will's phone?"

"Lauren ..." Patricia says.

"No." I'm usually a better liar. "Well ... yeah."

"What did you learn about my brother?"

"Not much of a texter."

"No kidding," Lauren says. "He hated texting. And trying to coax a conversation out of him on the phone wasn't any better. Monosyllable grunts. Painful. But if he was right in front of you, he would talk your ear off. Or more like, argue your ear off."

"Were you two close?" I ask.

"I wouldn't say close, but we didn't hate each other or anything. We basically lived in parallel universes. His was sports and guzzling beer with friends. Mine is working as a cashier at Save More Foods and the youth group and choir at church. Will never went to church. He thought religion was a bunch of crap. We didn't have much to talk about."

"Do you have siblings, Claire?" Patricia asks.

"Yes, my sister Belle."

"That's a pretty name," Patricia says.

Another long silence. Finally Patricia's strong mask begins to crack. Her bottom lip starts to quiver. "There was no warning, you see," she says. Lauren moves closer and puts her arm around her. "I never dreamed it would come to this." She pulls a Kleenex out of her sleeve and blows her nose. "He always seemed so vibrant, so happy in his life. His soccer team made the playoffs last season. Sure, he had to have an operation on his knee, but he was doing well, I thought. And he had a beautiful girlfriend. From the outside looking in, you would say he had it all."

"I'm sorry for your loss," I say. That sounds so incredibly corny. Patricia and Lauren deserve eloquent words I just can't seem to string together.

"Did you know that more people jump to their death

from the Lions Gate than any other bridge in the province?" Patricia says.

"Mom, I don't think Claire—"

"So many deaths, especially young people." Patricia sits up straight and leans closer to me, clutching her fist. "The coroner even made a recommendation that barriers or netting be installed on the bridge to stop people from jumping …" Her voice gets louder and louder. "That was in 2008, and there have been dozens more suicides since then and nothing has been done. And do you know why?"

"Mom—"

"The officials say it costs too much money. What is a life worth, you tell me that? What was my son's life worth?" She blows her nose again and composes something in her head while she looks at me. "Did you and Will talk? Did he say anything to you? Anything that would help us understand?"

Her sadness feels like the tip of a sharp knife stabbing me. "All he said to me was 'I'm sorry.'"

That does it. Patricia sobs into Lauren's shoulder. Seeing Lauren so caringly and gently comforting her mother makes me ache deep down. The word compassion pops into my mind.

"Please excuse me," Patricia says, and she leaves in a hurry to somewhere private.

Lauren and I look at each other awkwardly.

"We should have been the ones he said sorry to," Lauren says.

I nod. I now feel horrible about being the chosen one for Will's last words.

"Have the police talked with you and your mom?" I ask.

Lauren shrugs. "There was an autopsy—the impact killed him."

I see Will's body plummeting off the bridge about a hundred miles an hour.

"You know what happens to the body when you jump off a bridge that high?" she says. "All the internal organs tear loose and the ribs break and get shoved into the heart and lungs."

My head feels fuzzy and my stomach starts to churn. Lauren probably sees all the color drain from my face, so she changes the subject.

"Did he leave a note on his phone?" she asks.

I nod. Lauren grabs the phone, types in the passcode on the back. As she reads the note, I nervously play with the tassel on the corner of the pillow. She looks up at me. "That's it? What a self-centered asshole. I'm deleting it— my mom doesn't need to read this."

I'm now feeling way beyond uncomfortable. Lauren stares at me for a few seconds. "Everyone who comes here wants to see Will's room," she says. "You, too?"

Lauren leads me down a long hallway into Will's bedroom and watches me silently as I look around. The room is pretty much what I imagined. Two of the four walls are covered in FIFA posters of Real Madrid, United, and Chelsea.

"I've got his laptop, but I can't figure out any of his passwords to check his emails, and he was dismal at posting on social media." She seems to be as nosey as I am. A kindred spirit.

"Yeah, I checked email on his phone. Nothing much there. Same with Instagram."

Patricia must have cleaned Will's room. It doesn't smell like "boy" like Ty's room does. The bedspread doesn't have one wrinkle in it and there isn't one speck of dust on the dresser.

"He moved out about six months ago to some crappy basement apartment."

"Where?"

"Near Commercial Drive. Said he needed his own space. Probably so he and Danielle could have a love nest. When he lived here, Mom didn't let Danielle anywhere near this room. I never went to Will's new place, but Mom took him food all the time and, of course, gave him money. He barely took anything with him when he moved—except his soccer gear."

"Where did he work?"

"He leached off my mom, for the most part. When he needed extra beer money, he worked the odd construction job with my uncle."

His clothes still hang neatly in the closet. A few shirts beside carefully ironed jeans. Will's billowing white shirt after he jumped zips through my mind. I shake off the memory and pick up a photograph of Will and Danielle from the dresser, feel a pang of jealousy. How can I be jealous about a dead guy?

"I heard she's already dating," Lauren says. "And get this—it's a guy she met at Will's funeral. A law student Will knew through soccer. Talk about whacked." She takes the photo from me and inspects it closely.

"Not cool at all," I say. No way am I going to tell her I met Danielle.

"Mom loves Danielle. Well, Mom loves anything and anyone in Will's life, but especially the girlfriend. Mom thought for sure Will and Danielle were going to get married. Will didn't know it, but Mom was already researching community halls for the wedding reception." In a voice mocking her mother, "Because, you know, to get the right place you have to book a few years in advance." She sets the photo back on the dresser. "Danielle's only come around here once since Will died, right after the funeral. What a bitch."

"Agreed."

Lauren answers her ringing cellphone. "What's going on?" She says into the phone and trails off down the hall.

I can't help myself. I search through Will's dresser—

boxers, T-shirts, sporty workout clothes. Except for a pack of condoms at the bottom of his sock drawer, nothing's very interesting. I go through the desk drawer—pens, pencils, batteries, paper clips and elastics, a stapler, and ... a treasure. A most valuable player soccer medal with a photo of Will when he was about eight, smiling like the happiest kid on the planet, cut out into a circle and pasted on one side. I hear Lauren coming back to the room and slip the medal into my jacket pocket.

"Thanks for letting me see Will's room."

"It's part of the tour," Lauren says with a blank face.

I take one last look around. "Why do you think he did it?"

"God only knows—literally. All I know was he was really bummed out for quite a few months. His suicide note doesn't exactly explain details, does it?"

"Only that he was really messed up," I say.

"That's what sucks. I was hoping he said something to you that would somehow make things easier for my mom. You know, how sometimes it's easier to talk to a stranger than someone you know."

I do know. I think how easy it is for me to spill my guts

to Paul and write to Will, but so hard to talk to anyone close to me.

"I'd better get going," I say.

I follow Lauren down the hall. She opens the front door and I step out onto the porch. "Say goodbye to your mom for me," I say.

"Yeah, sorry about that. She's still pretty freaked out about everything."

"It must be so hard for her ... Bye." I start down the steps.

"I'm angry as hell at Will," Lauren says. I turn around. There are deep lines between her eyebrows. She talks through clenched teeth. "If you ask me, he's a selfish bastard for making my mom suffer so much. Do you know what a stigma it is, especially at church, if your son commits suicide? Will was the reason she got out of bed in the morning. This has destroyed her."

I nod and continue down the steps. I stick my hand in my pocket and feel the bumps on Will's soccer medal. I can't let him go. Not just yet.

Chapter 19

Kiki and I ride bikes toward Jericho Beach. The jagged black bumps of the mountains are outlined on the thick orange horizon. It's a warm summer night.

"Never partied with soccer players before," Kiki says, riding my mom's bike that she borrowed. "Fit, muscular, hunky guys. Oh, ya ..."

Kiki looks like a Bolivian mountain dweller in a toque with earflaps that have bright pink and orange woolen swirls. Even with the toque, it's easy to tell she's bald. She woohoos at the top of her lungs as she pedals ahead of me down the hill to the beach.

We lock up our bikes and follow the blaring electronic dance music, clinking bottles, and a blazing bonfire.

"I didn't know you were allowed fires on the beach," Kiki says.

"You're not."

When we arrive at a circle of partiers, I feel super awkward. Everybody looks at us as if we just stepped off a spaceship from planet Xoumia. But when a joint gets passed around, Kiki boldly steps right into the circle.

"Don't mind if I do," she says. She takes a long toke, coughs a few times, and hands me the joint. "This is what I'm talkin' about." More coughs.

I barely inhale. My throat burns and I burst into a coughing fit. Not cool. Not cool at all. I pass the joint to a girl beside me, who has caked-on makeup and a large gap between her front teeth.

Wasting no time, Kiki walks off and sits beside a cute guy on a log closer to the fire. The brown-haired guy from Will's soccer team strolls up, hooting and hollering and holding a can of Lucky Lager. Beer foam spews into the air. His eyes pop open wide when he sees me. I'm surprised he actually remembers who I am.

"You made it," he says, already pretty drunk, his breath

reeking of beer. "Someone get this girl a drink," he shouts. A stocky guy with a short bristle-brush Mohawk and a tattoo of an eagle on his arm hands me a beer. I'm thirsty, so I take a few big gulps. The cold bubbles feel good in my mouth.

"Um ... what's your name again?" Brown Hair asks.

"Claire," I say, and then burp loudly.

"Nice one. I'm Eddy, by the way." The made-up girl hands him the joint. He tokes deeply and passes it to me. I shake my head.

He's still inhaling as he talks. "Look, Claire, I hope you didn't come to this party just to talk about Will Szabo." He blows out the rest of the smoke and puts his arm around my shoulder. "In my opinion, the guy was so effing full of himself." He slurs his words. "I can guarantee you there're way more interesting things you and I can do tonight than discuss that arrogant prick."

"I'm not here to talk about Will—I'm here to party." I guzzle my beer until it's finished. More burps.

"Atta girl." Eddy opens the cooler and hands me another beer.

I am trying to take my mind off Will, even just for one

night. He's consumed almost every waking thought and commandeered most of my dreams. I've had enough. And Kiki desperately needed out of hospice for a night.

The beer has definitely kicked in. I look over at Kiki, who now has a beer in one hand and a joint in the other. She and the cute guy are laughing hysterically. I'm about to break free of Eddy's grasp, which started on my shoulder and then migrated to my ass, to go see what's making Kiki laugh so hard—but then the music changes to a song that's energizing, pumping, hypnotizing. I can't help myself. I start dancing like a crazy person, flailing my arms and kicking my legs, not a care in the world about who might think I'm looney tunes. Eddy joins in. In no time, almost everyone is dancing. Kiki is soon beside me. She's literally jumping for joy. I've never seen a smile so big. She and I hold hands as we dance, twirl each other around the fire, and laugh. I'm dizzy. Yell at the top of my lungs. Then I start howling like a wolf. Kiki does, too, and others follow.

It feels like hours slip by but I'm sure it's only minutes. Or maybe it feels like minutes but it's actually hours. I can't tell. All I know is the music keeps getting better and better.

I haven't felt so light, so carefree—so hooched up—ever. Kiki's now dancing with the cute guy and Eddy tries to keep his arms around my waist, even though I'm dancing my ass off.

I open my eyes. The house is dead quiet. I'm lying on my covers, fully dressed. From the crack open below my blind, it looks like the sun is just coming up. I have a pounding headache and a queasy stomach. The skin on my right ankle feels like a thousand wasps stung me. I pull up my jeans to look. My skin is bright red around the black ink of a tattoo of two stick figures holding hands. Both with bumps for breasts and dots for eyes, the mouths big U's. One of the figures has a few lines from the head to the shoulders, the other's head is just a round ball. Not hard to tell who the two are supposed to be. The scrawl, in amazingly neat printing, says, "We're here forever."

What a cliché—getting wasted at a party and waking up with a tattoo. I search my fuzzy brain, trying to remember the night—rewinding, fast forwarding, stopping at random scenes. Eddy and I making out on the beach. Him sticking his icy hand under my shirt. Oh, yeah, a guy with a tattoo gun and a lineup of partiers, but I don't remember being in that line. I remember the police cruiser's whoop-whoop siren and red flashing light. Two burly cops telling everybody to clear out. Makeup girl puking in the bushes. Cops handcuffing Mohawk guy and a mouthy girl with neon pink hair and a bullring piercing her nose, guiding them into the back of the cruiser. Riding bikes to a bus stop on Broadway, Kiki on the back of Mom's bike, singing off key to a song I never heard of, while the cute guy pedals. Dawson? Is that his name? How we got home from there is a total mystery.

Kiki's toque is on the floor. She's not on the bed with me, so I check the bathroom. She's curled up on the floor, her face as white as the toilet. I fall down on my knees and put my face close to hers to see if she's still breathing. Her eyes weakly flutter open.

"You scared the shit out of me," I say. "Are you okay?"

She lifts her head and her purplish lips slowly stretch out into a big smile. "Aside from barfing up the entire contents of my digestive system, I'm fan-fucking-tabulous. But my ankle hurts like hell."

I check her ankle, hidden under her jeans. She has an identical tattoo.

"My parents are going to kill me," I say. "Whose brilliant idea was it to get matching tattoos?"

"Guilty as charged."

"Is this a good idea for you? You know, considering your cancer and everything?"

"What? Like I might die or something?" She smiles as she closes her eyes and rests her bald head on the hard tile.

I slip one towel under her head, cover her with a clean bath sheet, and go back to bed.

I wake to bright sun in my eyes. Kiki's toque is gone and I hear voices and laughter from downstairs. I drag my body out of bed. My ankle is still shrieking in pain, but I put on socks so my parents won't see it.

In the kitchen, Mom and Dad clutch their coffee mugs and look amused while Kiki, now toqued, and Belle play "rock, paper, scissors" at the island.

"Belle, you can't always go with the rock. You've gotta switch it up," Kiki says. "Let's try again. One, two, three ..."

Belle chooses scissors to Kiki's paper. "Oh, man, you got me!" Kiki says. Belle laughs hysterically as she "cuts" Kiki's hand with her fingers. "Your sister's about to kick my ass," Kiki says to me.

"Yeah, I'm going to kick K-Kiki's ass," Belle says, all pleased with her victory. My parents' eyebrows rise in unison, right into their hairlines. I doubt they've ever heard Belle say the word "ass" before. As a matter of fact, neither have I.

"There's an omelet warming in the oven," Mom says.

"Thanks, but on behalf of my stomach, I'll take a pass." I put the kettle on for mint tea.

"Kiki said it was a fun beach party last night." Mom tries so hard to be hip and cool, but I'm sure my vulnerable developing brain keeps her awake at night. It sometimes keeps me awake, too.

"A little too much fun." Shouldn't have said that, knowing how anxious Mom already is.

"So I heard. Let me see." She looks down at my ankle. *Damn you, Kiki.* I take off my sock and pull up the leg of my jeans. Mom does her doctor thing and inspects it carefully. "Wash it with warm soapy water several times a day. Any yellow or green puss, or a bad smell, tell me."

"Oh, no, not again!" Kiki says, as Belle hits Kiki's scissors with her rock. Belle swallows her in a hug.

Kiki flops on my bed and closely inspects the tiny photo of Will taped on the soccer medal I looted from Will's room. To honor the day, I open iTunes on my laptop and play Kesha's song called "Hungover."

"I'd have both my legs cut off—my arms, too—if I could live even one year longer, and this guy offs himself because he had a sore knee." Kiki turns the medal over and over in her hand.

"It's more complicated than that. He lived and breathed soccer. Then he lost his game."

Kiki shakes her head. "Still, he had a choice whether to live or die. Some of us aren't so lucky." She puts the medal on my bedside table.

"But he lost hope."

I feel like such an idiot defending Will to Kiki. But I think I'm finally beginning to understand him. To have what you love—what you live for—taken away makes life feel pretty worthless. For me, it's like some deadly parasite has weaseled its way into my body and munched away all my inspiration from the inside out, leaving just an empty shell. The thought of never getting it back scares me more than anything. But does it scare me more than death?

"On the bright side of things, Dawson is seriously thinking about accommodating me, if you know what I mean." Kiki gives me an exaggerated wink and starts snooping around my room, checking out my bookshelf.

"You asked him to have sex with you?"

"I didn't exactly say, 'Hey Dawson, I'm dying, so how about a pity screw?' I just thought every guy would be interested in sex anytime, anywhere, and with pretty much anyone. But unfortunately, I had to meet a nice, sensitive guy." Kiki air-quotes the word "sensitive." "Dawson says he wants me to take some time to think about it. Make sure it'll be right for me. Geez."

"Sounds like a pretty decent guy, actually." I think of Ty. He's also a decent guy. Never pushes me into anything I'm not ready for.

"I had to tell Dawson time's a-tickin' away for me, which was probably a big turnoff. But I may never get to experience the real thing. Lucky I'm a master masturbator."

"Geez, Kiki."

"What?"

Uncensored-no-bullshit-take-me-or-leave-me-I-don't-have-much-time-left Kiki.

She checks out photos of Declan, Ty, Izzy, and me on my corkboard. "You must be able to hook me up with a guy friend or two." She unpins a photo of Ty at the beach, looking all tanned and hunky. "What about him? He's really hot."

"Sorry, he's got a girlfriend." I'm embarrassed about making out with Eddy last night and don't want Kiki to know about Ty and me. Not just yet, anyway.

"Bummer." She puts down Ty's photo and closely inspects my paintings hanging on the wall. "You do these?"

I nod.

"Do you know how good you are?"

I hesitate but nod again. Although I've got so much to learn, I am a good painter. At least, I was a good painter.

She searches through the music on my laptop. "Wanna help me with my funeral playlist? I should really start planning soon." She changes the song to Drake, "Over My Dead Body." Her voice cracks. "How perfect is that." I put my hand on her shoulder. She says, "You know what really sucks? I've finally met a friend here in Vancouver and I'll have to say adios way too soon."

I wrap her in a tight hug, like I'll never let her go. We stay that way for a very, very long time.

Kiki, Belle, and I say our goodbyes on the front porch. Belle plants a sloppy kiss on my cheek while our parents wait in the car.

"Why don't you come, Claire? Why not?" Belle says.

"I'll visit your group home another day, Belle. I'm not feeling that great right now."

"Too much beer, right, C-Claire? Beer?" She lets out a husky laugh.

"You got it, Bella-Belle." I brush a strand of hair off her face. The skin on her cheek is soft.

Kiki says, "Probably leaving hospice soon. Even

though my mom and I live in a crapper of an apartment on Kingsway, don't be a stranger."

"Time to go, K-Kiki." Belle points to the car.

As Kiki and Belle walk down the path, Ty drives up. He gets out of the van, carrying one long-stemmed red rose. He waves at my parents, high-fives Belle, and lets her chase him around the front yard for a few minutes. Kiki turns to me and smirks before she gets into the car. Busted.

Chapter 20

Ty's blond curls flip-flop as he takes the front steps two at a time. He hands me the rose. "If you'd listened to my voicemails or read any of my texts, you'd know I've apologized about a million times for whatever it was I said to upset you."

Usually when I lay eyes on him, it's like a dragon breathes fire on me from head to toe. But now there's only a small puff of smoke rising from the dragon's snout.

"I may have screwed up, but you're not exactly an angel, either," he says. "You clam up, don't tell me what you want or what you need. And I'm no mind reader."

I do know that. I shrug.

"Still all my fault?" he says.

I shrug again.

"What am I supposed to do if you won't talk to me?"

Another shrug.

"Wanna go for a drive?" he asks.

"No, I don't." My inner bitch explodes. "All we ever do together is drive around in your van and end up at Spanish Banks. Except maybe for the odd detour to the cemetery."

"So not true."

"Yes, it *is* true. We're so predictable, Ty. Tell me when we've done anything I've ever suggested, like hiking the Grouse Grind, checking out a new exhibit at the art gallery, going for a picnic at Lighthouse Park, or swimming at a lake?"

"You know I'm a sinker." He hangs his head like a puppy caught chewing a shoe. "What do you want to do then? Anything."

"To be honest ... I just want to go back to bed. I'm beat. Maybe I'll see you tomorrow at the cc."

"Yeah. Maybe." By the sound of his voice and the look on his face, I have my doubts.

"So why did he do it?" Izzy says, disappearing under the table with her bucket and a cloth. I meet her under the table and wipe down the other table legs.

"I hacked into his cellphone, read his texts and emails, listened to his voice mail, creeped his Instagram, talked to his family and friends, even his girlfriend. Nothing else makes sense," I say.

"No one would kill themselves for something that lame," Izzy says. "I mean, just because he injured himself and didn't get a university scholarship? Or couldn't play soccer on the team he wanted to? Come on. I'd believe it if his one true love—his soul mate—died of a brain tumor or else left him forever to work for the Red Cross in Somalia, and he knew he would never, ever meet anyone like her again. Or maybe if he had a repressed memory of being sexually abused as a kid by a teacher, a priest, or a soccer coach that haunted him, and there was no therapy that could heal such a deep, painful wound."

"I miss you, Izzy."

"I miss you too, Claire-bear. And I know someone else has been missing you lately, too."

"Ty came over yesterday. We talked."

"Yeah, he came over to Declan's right after. Mumbled something like, 'What's wrong with Spanish Banks?' Did you guys break up or something?"

"I don't think so. Maybe. Who knows?" Did Ty and I break up for good this time?

My shift is over. To avoid biking over any bridges, I take the long way to St. Michael's through crazy traffic—West 4th, which turns into 6th, which turns into 2nd, to Main Street, and then north to Strathcona.

It feels emptier at hospice, knowing Kiki's no longer staying here. I look down at the still stinging tattoo on my ankle. "We're here forever." That is, unless I get laser removal. Elvis isn't here to greet me, either, wagging his tail, begging for pats. I wander down the hallway toward Paul's office and look in the family room, where the woman was curled up with her two small children. The name on the door of the next room says *Julius Schultz*—Mom's patient. I open the door. Julius's skin is the color of burnt butter. His eyes are shut and his mouth gapes open, trying to suck in as much air as possible. Tubes come out of his nose and arms. He's so wrinkled and dry, it looks like he has rhino skin. He opens one eye.

"Knock knock," he says, choking out the words.

I come up to the side of his bed.

"Who's there?" I say.

"Aardvark." He tries to focus on me.

"Aardvark who?"

Julius wheezes. "Aardvark a million miles for one of your smiles." As usual, Julius cracks up at his own joke. The laughing ends in a coughing fit. I'm worried the joke is going to kill him. But he closes his eyes and his breath settles back into a gasping rhythm. I leave him to sleep. In the hallway, Paul walks toward me.

"I need a fix," he says, jittering his body like a junkie.

At the ice cream shop, he orders us what he says is the *pièce de résistance*: a super scoop mocha fudge cheesecake with hazelnuts—in a waffle cone, of course.

"How did you end up working at hospice?" I ask.

"It wasn't part of my plan, that's for sure. Long story or the abridged version?"

"I'll go for the long story." I take a bite of the sweetest, most delicious thing I've ever put in my mouth. Ever. And I mean *ev-er*.

"Once upon a time, about eight years ago, I was a lawyer in Toronto, making the big bucks, driving fancy cars, with a ridiculously large house in the city and a condo in the Caymans. Remember I told you life has to slap me upside the head to get my attention? Well, this was more like a sucker punch.

"My wife and I threw a big party one night. All the mucky-mucks were there—big-shot lawyers, presidents of big prestigious corporations—and even the Premier of the province showed up. I remember looking across the sea of people and thinking, with all this power and money right under my roof, I must be the hottest shit around."

Paul pauses to gather his thoughts and have a bite of his waffle cone. I lick the melting bits of fudge and nuts from mine.

"My wife and I drank way too much fine wine and single malt Scotch that night. Both of us passed out—sound asleep—and didn't hear our three-year-old daughter get up. Sophie was a night wanderer, so we always had to keep a close eye on her. Well, most of the time it was Pearl, our nanny, who kept an eye on Sophie, but Pearl had gone back to the Philippines to visit her family. My wife and I found Sophie in the morning. She'd drowned in our swimming pool, right below our bedroom window."

"Ho-ly crap!" I say, feeling like *I* just got sucker punched.

"My life started to fall apart piece by piece. My wife and I couldn't get past blaming one another, so the marriage ended soon after. I became physically and psychologically paralyzed and was in such a crisis that a three-month leave from work turned into six months, which then turned into a year. My fellow law partners then politely asked me to cash in and leave the firm. To make a long story even longer … after much soul searching and counseling to try to make meaning of my tragedy, as clichéd as it sounds, I gave away pretty much everything I owned. I needed a clean slate, as far away from my old life as possible. When I heard about a job opening for the Executive Director of St. Michael's Hospice in Vancouver, I thought: what have I got to lose? Why not give it a try? I certainly know something about death and grief. As it turns out, I think I found my calling."

"How did you ... um ... I mean, like ... how did you ... get over your little girl's death?"

"I'll never fully get over Sophie's death. At first I asked all the usual questions. Why Sophie? Why me? I'm not meant to know everything, and that pisses me right off because I'm a know-it-all kind of guy. I've come to realize that if there's meaning in life, there also has to be meaning in suffering. They go hand in hand."

"I get what you're saying. Will Szabo offed himself because he didn't think he was good enough to play soccer in the big leagues like he'd hoped."

"Sounds like suffering to me."

The bell on the shop door rings. Three people enter and sit at the table next to us.

"How do I stop feeling like a zombie and start feeling myself again?"

Paul leans closer to me. "By staring your trauma right in the face."

"How do I do that?"

Paul wipes a drip of ice cream off his chin. "Take soldiers

who suffer from Post-Traumatic Stress Disorder. After a gradual build-up with some pretty intensive counseling, a new virtual reality therapy has them relive their traumatic experiences. They wear virtual reality glasses or some kind of head-mounted device that simulates a battlefield—machine guns firing, bombs going off. That kind of thing. Rather than burying their fears, they walk right toward them. I'm not saying you need virtual reality therapy, but what I am saying is you have to deal with whatever you're experiencing head on. You can't avoid it."

"So by talking about the suicide with you, I'm facing it head on?"

"Talking to me might be enough, but we have a deal, right? If our mocha-fudge-cheesecake-waffle-cone therapy sessions aren't helping, you're going to dial it up a notch and see a professional therapist. Agreed?"

I nod.

"Claire, it seems to me you're hanging on to Will and the trauma you experienced. But it's not about him anymore—he made his choice. It's about you now. I love the quote by Mark Twain: 'The two most important days in your life are the day you are born and the day you find out why.'"

Those words sink into every pore of my body.

Paul and I say our goodbyes in the hospice foyer amongst the tropical plants and squawking parrots. "Shall we continue to explore our collective existential crises next week?" he says.

I reply in my best British professorial accent, "Nothing like thrashing out the meaning of life and death over a super scoop."

"Hear, hear," Paul says, and gives me a big hug.

I walk down the corridor to Julius's room and stop at the door. Mom is sitting beside his bed, holding his hand. Julius's breathing is sporadic. He looks unconscious, his eyes glued shut.

"Mom?"

"Claire, what are you doing here?" Her eyes are red.

"Visiting a friend."

"Not Kiki, I hope."

"No, just someone I met who works here," I say.

Mom turns back to Julius. We're quiet for a few

minutes, listening to him gasp for every breath. "There's nothing more I can do to help him," she says. "And I can't shake the feeling I've failed somehow."

"Julius loves you like crazy, and you did everything you could for him." I sit on the edge of her chair and wrap my arm around her shoulder. "None of us are meant to live forever, Mom."

Mom offers to throw my bike in the back of her car, but I make a decision. Like Paul says, it's time to face my ordeal head on. I ride my bike fast through the downtown streets, legs pumping hard. I'm flying as if the bike tires aren't even connecting to the pavement. And I have the sweet taste of mocha fudge cheesecake in my mouth. I finally get on West Georgia, the road that will take me right to the Lions Gate Bridge.

As I approach the bridge, that same old stomach-churning, sweaty, faint feeling hits me hard. Do soldiers wearing the virtual reality glasses feel the same way going through their human videogame? People walk and cycle on the bridge walkway as traffic zooms by on the road.

Although I feel wobbly, I ride onto the sidewalk without getting off my bike. Or puking.

In the distance, I spot the place where Will jumped. I try to keep my eyes on it as I weave around walkers and other cyclists. I get closer. I can see a memorial for Will with photos and bouquets of wilted brown flowers. The sweet taste in my mouth turns sour, like I just bit into a lemon.

Two tourists with cameras dangling from their necks walk side by side, taking up the whole sidewalk. A cyclist in spandex yells at them. He flips them the finger when he's forced to weave around them and scrape the railing, squashing the wilted bouquet. I don't want to lose momentum, so I veer closer to the road. I make it around the tourists just as a skateboarder rockets toward me. I swerve, but the skateboarder crashes into me. I fly off my bike. Tires screech.

And then I black out.

Chapter 21

Voices.

Call 9-1-1

Smell of dirt. Car exhaust.

For Chrissake, someone stop the traffic.

Eyes open. Blur of whizzing cars.

Eyes close.

Sirens. Tires screech to a stop. More voices.

Can you hear me?

Warm liquid oozes out my nose. Snot? Blood?

What's your name?

More sirens.

What date is your birthday? Can you wiggle your toes for me?

Head throbs.

Fingers on my neck. Pulse. Am I still alive?

Eyes open.

Gray clouds.

Where do you hurt? Can you tell me?

Head pounds.

Eyes close.

Stretcher. Ambulance. Siren.

Eyes open. Ceiling tiles and lights zip by.

Dizzy.

Claire, can you hear me? Claire?

Everything goes black.

I'm floating out of my body. Is this what dying feels like?

My mind turns into a jumble of terrifying dreams. Exploding bombs. Bodies flying in all directions. A glass floor shatters beneath me with every step I take. Scary dolls with knives chase me. A surgeon pulls my beating heart out of my chest while I'm awake. Someone pushes me off the Lions Gate Bridge.

My parents are here. Dad's voice is soft and low, as usual, so I can't hear what he's saying. Mom's asking the doctor all the medical questions, but her voice sounds shaky. *Mom and Dad, I'm still here. Don't give up on me.*

I only catch a word or two in each sentence. But most of the conversation between Mom and the doctor sounds like they're speaking in code.

"T-B-I ... intracranial ..."

"Diffuse axonal ... M-R-S"

"... C-T ... M-R-I."

I want to move. Let them know I'm still here, but it's as if my eyelids are pasted shut. They probably think I'm a vegetable.

Other words float into my ears.

"Severe impact" ... "spinal cord severed" ... "paralysis" ... "quadriplegic."

I hear the doctor say she's sorry. I hear a woman crying. Probably my mom. My head is all light and floaty. I can't feel my body. Can't move my arms or legs. Paralysis. Quadriplegic. I might as well be a vegetable.

Curtain swooshes. Machines beep. Wheels click and squeak across the floor.

"How you doin' today, Claire? I'm Malcom."

I try to open my eyes but it's too much effort.

He smells like cinnamon and cloves and his accent sounds Jamaican. "You banged up your head pretty good, but you're going to be just fine. You know that, right? You gotta just hang in there."

I kind of doubt it, Malcom. As far as I can tell, I'm breathing, eating, and peeing through tubes, and I'm paralyzed from the neck down. I'd call that not all right.

Malcom fusses with things around me while he talks. "What kind of music do you like? I'll get your parents to bring some in for you. Get you some big-ass headphones. Doubt you'd like my sappy tunes. I'm a sucker for female pop stars ... Lady Gaga, Adele ... and Beyoncé is not only an amazing performer, she's just plain hot. Know who I like the best? Wait for it ... Celine Dion." He hums the theme song from *Titanic*. I almost forgive him for Beyoncé, but Celine Dion? Seriously?

Clanking tray. "This stuff I'm giving you will make you fly to the moon and back." I don't know what Malcom gives me, but he's right—I feel like I'm levitating. He wraps his large hand around the top of my head, maybe to keep me grounded for a few minutes longer. He doesn't move his hand for a long time. Being touched has never felt so good. Soon I'm sailing out of my body and tripping in another dimension.

The hospital room is dim. Tubes snake out of gasping machines. I get out of my hospital bed, remove the hoses and needles stuck all over my body. In the hallway, symphony music plays. Stage lights shine on nurses crisscrossing the hallway like ballet dancers, doing pirouettes and pliés and arabesques while balancing trays of medicine. When I raise my hand to get their attention, the ceiling and walls turn to glass and shatter around the dancing nurses. It doesn't stop them. I stick out my hand again and the shattered glass coalesces back into place. Two Ninjas, in black karate gear and face masks, join the ballet dance, lurching all stealthily, Ninja-style. I try to dance but I can't move my legs or arms.

When it's just you and your brain, you've got all the time in the world to think. In fact, that's all you can do (except when you're tripping out on the drugs, and then all you can do is be an actor in a bizarre or terrifying Sci-Fi or horror film). I can't help but think of the irony in all this. Paul challenged me to face my trauma. I faced it head on, all right. Now look at me. I'm hopeless. I sink deeper and deeper into a place that I don't know I can crawl out of. If machines are keeping me alive, and if I can never be myself again—truly myself—what's the point of living?

One thing that gave me hope for my future. When that was taken away, there wasn't much left to hang around for.

I lose track of time. When I open my eyes, it's a blur. Is it day or night? Mom's reading to me. Poems, I think. I don't recognize the words. Something about light through a crack. Leonard Cohen, maybe? I try to say something, but my tongue feels about ten times too big for my mouth. There's a faint scent of paint thinner. Dad is obviously here, too. Both tell me they love me. I'm taking them away from their lives, their work ... from Belle. Where is Belle? *I miss you Bella-Belle.* Kisses on my forehead. Gentle caresses on my cheek.

Malcom must have found those big-ass headphones because Alice Merton's song, "Roots," is blasting. Or am I just dreaming?

Have days gone by? Weeks? Months?

Ty, Izzy, and Declan are in my room. I can sense their presence before any of them says a word. Their shapes are like an out-of-focus picture. They talk softly, as if in a church. I hear a quacking sound and know it's Izzy, blowing her nose. When she has a cold, Ty calls her Daisy Duck. Somebody touches my face. Maybe Ty. Maybe Izzy. Chairs scraping on the floor, footsteps moving away. *Hey, guys, it's not exactly party time in here, but please don't leave.*

Different air in the room. I see a dark shape float around.

But whoever it is, they don't say a word. Same curtain swooshing, tires squeaking. *That's not you, is it, Malcom?* My body's being flipped over like a fish on the deck of a boat, the smell of bleach on the sheets as they flap-flap-flap into place. I'm turned over on my other side. Then on my back. Cool water over my face. Dried with a towel that's about as soft as sandpaper. I'm soon tripping back into another terrifying parallel universe.

God and the Devil battle it out for my soul, but it's all in black and white anime. God throws bolts of lightning and the Devil stops them with his iron wristbands. The Devil responds by shooting fire from his fingertips. God snuffs out the flames in his eternal fountain of water. It turns into a slow motion Ultimate Fighter Championship match—punching, kicking, blood and sweat spraying. Both God and the Devil have deep gashes on their faces. They spit out teeth. I don't know who might win. God and the Devil morph into Kiki and Will arguing at the end of my bed. I can't tell if Kiki is God and Will is the Devil, or the other way around. Kiki wears a baseball cap with fake black braids hanging down. Will is pretty easy to look at in his soccer jersey and jeans. His blue eyes are mesmerizing.

Will says, "Claire can't breathe, eat, or even piss on her own. She'll be crapping in a plastic bag attached to her body for the rest of her life. What kind of life is that?"

"At least she'll be alive." Kiki plays with one of the braids.

"She's a quadriplegic, for Chrissakes. Claire's got an out here. I vote she does what's best for her and everyone else in her life, and shuts herself down." Will sits in a wheelchair by the bed.

"What? Like you? Just because you weren't going to become some hotshot superstar soccer player?"

"Yes, like me. When life gives you lemons, you get the fuck out." His hands are on the wheels and he rolls the chair back and forth.

"You should have tamed your over-inflated ego, put on some reality glasses, and just got on with it."

"I could have. But I didn't want to. That's why I ended it."

"You suck," Kiki says.

"You suck." Will's now doing wheelies.

"Life is a gift and you squandered it." Kiki takes off

the baseball cap. The braids are attached. I can see inside her head. Tiny sparks fly from different parts of her brain when she speaks.

"Yeah, life's a gift when it works out. When it doesn't, it's a living nightmare. Look at Claire. She'll never be able to paint, ever again—her one true purpose for existing on this planet."

"She has other reasons—her family, friends, a brilliant future. Besides, knowing Claire, she'll paint with her mouth if she has to."

"You've gotta be kidding me. You've seen her paintings; you know how talented she is. You really think she'd ever be satisfied painting with a brush sticking out of her mouth?"

"Life is more than what we do or what we're good at. It's who we are and who we love."

"What a bunch of fluffy bullshit." Will gets out of the wheelchair and inspects a bag of fluid hanging from a pole. "If we can't fulfill our main purpose for being on this Earth, it's time to check out, and stop taking up precious room and resources. You get that, right, Claire?"

Suddenly, Will and Kiki peer right over me on either

side of the bed. Do I want to live? As a quadriplegic, I won't really be me anymore. I'll be just a carcass, a pile of bones. I'll be a miserable human being, living like that.

"Death isn't so bad, Claire," Will says. "It's like being on the best drugs ever. If you think you can be creative on Earth, just wait for the afterlife. It's bloody amazing what portals will open up for you."

"Don't listen to him, Claire. He's a loser. His head was so far up his ass, he didn't know what he had when he was alive."

"Come on. Do you really want to paint with a brush in your mouth for the rest of your life?"

"You can do it, Claire. You'll see."

"Let's see right now." Will opens my mouth and sticks paint brushes down my throat, one at a time. I'm choking.

Buzzers and alarms go off, anxious footsteps rush into my room.

Do not resuscitate! Please, just let me go. I'm ready ...

Chapter 22

A blur of movement. Like glass smeared with paintbrush strokes. It makes me dizzy. The fuzziness slowly comes into focus. Are my eyes open? Am I still dreaming? Or tripping? The light is dim. All I can see are beeping robots with flashing red eyes and long strands of pasta straggling out their mouths in a jumbled mess. I try to read a sign hanging above one of the machines, but the letters scramble like a train station departure board.

How much time has passed? An hour? A day? My eyes are pried open one at a time. A bright light blinds me. I focus enough to see a woman with a galaxy of freckles covering her pale skin. She snaps off the light. I blink a few times.

"Claire, I'm Doctor Saunders. Can you hear me?"

My mouth refuses to make words so I try to nod. But that doesn't work, either.

"You're in the Intensive Care Unit at St. Paul's hospital. You were in a bike accident and sustained a serious concussion. If things have been a bit foggy, it's because you have been heavily sedated for the past few days. But everything's looking really good, and I'm pleased with your recovery."

Everything's looking good? What's she talking about? I'm paralyzed. I close my eyes and try to remember the accident. I remember being at St. Michael's ... saw my mom in Julius's room ... then I left on my bike to go downtown. After that, it's a blank canvas.

How long did I sleep? I open my eyes. My parents are by my bed. I want to reach out to them, but I can't move. Where's Belle? Light slowly dissolves into blackness.

I wake again. My parents are still there but in different clothes. A different day? A different week? I open my mouth. They wait expectantly, hoping I'll say something. But I can't coax the words that are stuck in my brain down to my vocal cords. I want to tell them I'm sorry for putting them through all the worry. And sorry for what's to come. Instead, I slip back into my druggy haze.

Malcom is at the end of my bed, writing something on a chart and singing "The Power of Love." He doesn't have dreadlocks and he isn't wearing a woven Rasta hat the colors of the Jamaican flag as I imagined. What a stereotyper I am. He's tall and muscular in his maroon scrubs—clean cut—with a shaved head and bushy black eyebrows.

"Celine Dion?" I say in the most disapproving tone I can muster. "You kidding me?" My voice is all wheezy and crackly.

Malcom looks up from his clipboard and breaks into a huge smile. "Come on now, girl. You tell me what other singer has a five-octave range? Celine is the undeniable queen of pop."

"Queen of shlock." I clear the crud out of my throat.

"Now that hurt real bad, Claire."

"You smell like apple pie," I say.

Malcom lets out a booming laugh. "So that's why the ladies are always fallin' all over me."

That very short conversation wears me out. Malcom's face stretches and distorts, like I'm looking at him through the bottom of a glass.

"Don't go away, now. I've got to let a whole bunch of people know Sleeping Beauty has finally decided to grace us with her words."

I close my eyes.

Mom gently strokes my head. Dad is behind her with his hand around her shoulder.

"Hey, sweetie, how are you?" Mom says.

"Alive." I have a desperate feeling that's not going to be good enough.

"You gave us quite the scare," Dad says. I've never seen him this emotional.

"Sorry."

"I spoke with Dr. Saunders and, from the latest scans, she thinks it should be smooth sailing from here," Mom says.

"Smooth sailing?" I say.

"I know you must feel overwhelmed and it will take some time. But you're going to make a full recovery," Mom says.

"How can you say that, Mom? I'm paralyzed."

My parents share a look.

"You don't have to protect me. I heard the doctor. She said something about the impact of the crash severing my spinal cord. I know I'm a quadriplegic."

Mom grasps my hand. What? I can feel it. I squeeze back.

"Honey, that was someone next to you in the Emergency ward. A poor guy who had a motorcycle accident. You must have heard the doctor talking to his family."

Dad touches both my feet—I can feel them, too. I wiggle my toes. I bend my knee, but it hurts like hell. In fact, my whole body is starting to slowly wake up and complain bitterly.

"But I haven't been able to move my arms or legs this whole time."

"You were pretty agitated when you first came to the hospital. Common for head trauma patients. You had to be restrained so you wouldn't pull out IVs, ventilator tubes, and so you wouldn't kick the nurses."

"But why couldn't I *feel* my body?"

"Maybe because you were convinced you were paralyzed. The brain is pretty impressionable after a serious trauma," Mom says.

I wonder if this is just another dream. But it all feels so real.

"It's a miracle you didn't break any bones, but you're pretty bruised up, especially your left side and your back. The medication will help, but you'll be sore and achy for quite some time."

"Where did the accident happen?"

Dad clears his throat, tugs on his ear. "The Lions Gate."

What was I doing there? I can't remember a thing.

"When can I see Belle?"

Dad says, "Let's wait until you're home and feeling better. Right now, you need calm and lots of rest."

It takes me three days to be able to sit up for any length of time. And sitting up makes me so nauseous I become a barfing machine. Another two days to stand without almost passing out. I'm finally ready to walk to the bathroom to have a shower.

"Did I really kick you?" I ask Malcom as he disconnects all the needles and tubes that are stuck into almost every orifice of my body.

"Yeah, but with my lightning quick reflexes, I grabbed your leg before you could do any serious damage. Can't say the same for Bonita, the night nurse. You literally kicked her butt."

"Oh, man. Was she mad?"

"That's why you were all tied up. But don't worry. She left for Costa Rica on holidays. You'll be out of the ICU before she gets back."

Malcom takes my arm and guides me as I shuffle into the bathroom. My body feels like I've been beaten up by Doctor Doom. Mom forgot to mention that along with a bruised brain, I also banged up my face pretty badly. My nose is scraped and scabbed. Both my eyes probably started out black but have turned shades of purple with rings the color of pea soup. Definitely not going to win any Miss Universe competitions. I slowly slip off my hospital gown and stand under the shower. The water stings my bruised and battered skin.

After my shower, I ask Malcom to take me to Jason Beckman's room, the guy paralyzed in the motorcycle accident. The mask over his bruised face gurgles and hisses. A machine with squiggly lines and flashing lights beeps. He's unconscious; probably tripping out on the same drugs I was given. I rest my hand on the top of his head, gently stroke his matted hair with my fingers. The bullet I dodged hit this guy right in the spine.

Later that afternoon, I wake up to Izzy, Declan, and Ty's clomping footsteps. Izzy, wearing a white mini-skirt and a T-shirt with multi-colored geometric shapes, carries a bouquet of flowers, which I'm pretty sure she pilfered from someone's front yard. Her little sprigs are seriously dwarfed by the enormous bouquet of flowers on my dresser sent With Love from Tessa, Celia, and the CC gang.

Declan takes one look at me and bursts out laughing. Ty looks pale. He hangs back, hands in his pocket.

"Shut up," Izzy snaps at Declan. She sits on the bed

beside me and hands me the bouquet. The sweet scent of the flowers is a nice change from hospital stench.

"Didn't you guys get the memo?" I say. "It's World Zombie Day."

"I've got to get pictures of this," Declan says as he pulls out his iPhone and takes a few photos of me. "Snapchat and Instagram won't know what hit them." I stick out my tongue and cross my eyes for the full effect. Ouch! That hurt.

Izzy stands to make room for Ty. He sits on the bed and takes my hand. "How long are you in here for?"

"I begged my mom to pull some strings. They're sending me home, rather than moving me to another ward. My mom's going to take some time off work. She's a doctor, for crying out loud. I'm pretty sure she can handle things from here."

"We came just after your accident, but they wouldn't let us into your room. Wouldn't even let us peek through the window," Izzy says.

"Really? I was sure you were in my room. I even heard you."

"Must have been the drugs talking," Declan says.

Perfect timing. Fiona, the nurse who shares me with Malcom, comes in the room. "Sorry to break up the party, but it's time for your meds, Claire."

Izzy and Declan say their goodbyes and file out of the room. Ty stays. The nurse hangs by the doorway to give us some privacy.

"You scared the living shit out of me." Ty chokes on his words. His eyes well up.

"Sorry." I reach up and wipe away a tear that snuck down his cheek.

"Maybe I'll come over when you get home," Ty says.

"You'd better."

He takes a long look at my face. "You'd make a great extra in a *Resident Evil* movie. You wouldn't even need makeup." He laughs and cries at the same time, wipes his face with his shirtsleeve.

"Ha ha, very funny."

He kisses me very gently on the lips. One of his tears lands on my face.

When I get home, all I can do is crawl into bed and stay

there. For days. On end. If I were on a reality TV show like *Big Brother*, it would have been the most mind-numbing episode ever.

MEDIUM CLOSE-UP: Claire lying on her back, sleeping.

CUT IN: Claire turns onto her right side as she sleeps.

OVER-THE-SHOULDER SHOT: Claire staggers to the bathroom to barf.

MEDIUM SHOT: Claire's mother takes her blood pressure. Takes her temperature. Checks her eyes. Listens to her chest with a stethoscope.

CUT IN: Claire turns over onto her left side. Still sleeping.

EXTREME CLOSE-UP: Slobber strings out her mouth in long thin threads and pools on her pillow.

OVER-THE-SHOULDER SHOT: Claire staggers to the bathroom to pee.

WIDE SHOT: Back to bed. Claire sleeps on her stomach, snoring.

CUTAWAY: Claire's mom brings her something for her pain. Claire swallows a small white pill with water.

POINT-OF-VIEW SHOT: On the ceiling, Claire sees an

image of herself, in front of her easel, staring at a blank canvas.

At the end of my three-week sleeping and puking marathon, I wake to the smell of food cooking. It actually smells appetizing and doesn't send me running for the bathroom.

In the kitchen, Dad's flipping eggs and Mom's reading the newspaper.

"Well, well, look who's finally up," Dad says.

"Yup, I'm finally vertical."

Mom flips a newspaper page. "Need anything for pain?"

"Nope."

"Still nauseous?" Dad says.

"Nope."

"Then you're ready for my breakfast extraordinaire?"

"Bring it on," I say. "Well, maybe just the toast."

"Coming right up," he says.

"Mom, how's Julius?"

"He died when you were in the hospital."

I go to her. "I'm sorry." Wrap my arm around her shoulder.

She nods. "As you once told me, no one gets out of this alive."

I kiss her on the cheek. "When can I see Belle?"

Chapter 23

Wearing the Bolivian woolen hat, Kiki yells "hey" and waves at me as she strides toward the bus stop where I'm waiting.

"What a coincidence. I was just coming over to your house," she says. I don't think the color in her cheeks is painted on, which surprises me.

"I've missed you," I say, and give her a big hug.

"I texted and called you a bajillion times. I thought you were trying to ditch me, so I asked Paul if he knew what was going on, but of course he didn't. Then I finally talked to your mom. I feel so terrible for not visiting you in the hospital."

"Considering I was in la la land for about four days, and barely coherent for another five days, I don't think you missed too much."

"I couldn't believe it when I heard."

"Strange, eh? But I'll live."

"Yeah, lucky you," Kiki says.

"Sorry."

"Don't be sorry. It's the tiptoeing around everything that really sucks ass. Where you off to?"

"Langley, for lunch at Belle's new group home. You have to come with me. My dad was going to, but he had to go to a meeting." I miss Belle like crazy. Although I begged my parents to bring her home right after I got out of the hospital, it was a good call on their part to wait until I was feeling better. Belle's over-the-top energy would not have helped my throbbing headaches.

"I'm in. Would love to see Belle."

The late August breeze shakes leaves that are almost ready to fall off the trees. We wait for the bus with an elderly couple holding hands, a woman with her baby in a sling, and a group of guys checking their electronic devices. Kiki pulls her scarf tighter around her neck.

"How's it going? Feeling any better?" she asks.

"My head still feels like it's in a vise grip. Squeezing

tighter and tighter. I've had trouble concentrating on anything. I sleep. And sleep. And sleep. Tried to watch *Resident Evil: Afterlife*, but slept through the whole movie." That night, Ty covered me with a blanket and I woke up on the couch in the TV room the following afternoon.

"You slept through *Resident Evil*? Are you kidding me?"

"And my bitch-o-meter has been *w-a-ay* off the charts. My poor parents. That's why I've been waiting to call you."

"Yeah, your mother warned me you might bite my head off." The bus comes and Kiki and I get on and sit at the very back. "Anything else?"

"Not so bad now. When I first got home, it was vomit, barf, puke, dry heaves. And ... repeat."

"Sounds a lot like chemo." A toddler in the seat in front of us peeks over. Kiki sticks out her tongue, which makes the kid pop down out of sight. It becomes a game, and soon we see two eyes peer over the seat.

"Speaking of ... How are you? You look good," I say.

"Well, here's the weird thing. Every time the docs try to give me my final death sentence, I seem to go into yet another impossible remission. They stroke their beards, mumble between themselves, shake their heads in amazement."

"It's because you have hope, you want to live. You're fighting to live." I'm starting to believe some people might actually have a choice about whether to hang on to life or let go.

"Hey, I even quit smoking ... Nothing's forever, but I'll be bugging you for a little while longer. We got lots of shit to do together."

"Lots and lots of shit." We both laugh. I remember my strange dream with Will and Kiki arguing. It's still so vivid in my mind and I wonder if, on some level, it actually happened. As much as I've tried to understand why, I can't shake the feeling Will gave up on life way too soon, while Kiki is clinging to life with every last cell in her body.

The front door of the group home flies open. "C-C-Claire!" Belle wails like an out-of-tune siren and runs into my arms, almost knocking me to the ground.

"Bella-Belle," I hug her as hard as I can without hurting myself. I want to hate this neighborhood. I want to argue with my parents that the group home is a crappy place for

Belle to live. But Belle's place looks just like all the others on the block—the house and yard are neat and tidy, and pink pansies cascade out of two large hanging baskets on either side of the front door.

Belle envelops Kiki. I'm afraid Kiki might break. "Hey, bellisima Belle. What's shakin'?"

Two girls around Belle's age watch us from the door with big smiles. One is as Down syndrome pudgy as Belle with big eyes. The other girl, with long blonde braids, looks as excited to see us as Belle is.

"Come, come ..." Belle pulls Kiki and me into the house, past the other girls, through the living room, down a hallway into her bedroom.

"My room. See?" Belle says.

"Wow, cool, Belle," I say.

"Nice digs," Kiki says.

Belle's bedroom is tiny compared to her room at home, but she's managed to crowd in her desk, dresser, and bed. The bed is covered in a mountain of stuffed animals.

"Did you paint these?" Kiki asks me, looking at two paintings hanging on the wall.

"D-Daddy painted this one," says Belle, pointing to a small painting of a tree filled with tiny birds. "Claire did this one." The picture I painted for Belle a few years ago is of a wooden swing with yellow rope hanging from a tree.

"Embarrassing. Note to self: paint a decent picture for your sister," I say.

"Are you back painting yet?" Kiki asks.

I shake my head.

Belle has a corkboard covered mostly with pictures of our family in various combinations. The one I like best was taken in Mexico during Spring Break. The four of us are posing on the beach, wet hair, and smiles as bright as the sunshine. At this moment, I wish I could teleport back in time. Life seemed so much simpler back then.

"Come." Belle pulls us from her bedroom, down a long hall. The kitchen is large for the size of the house. The girl with the braids grates cheese at the island. The group home worker, in her early twenties, supervises. She turns to us.

"Hey, Belle, aren't you going to introduce us?" she asks.

"C-Claire's my sister. She's my sister."

"Hi, I'm Kiki."

"Welcome—I'm Maya." The group home worker holds out her hand for us to shake. She has sparkly hazel eyes and a long brown ponytail. A small tasteful ring in her nose. "This is Cicily," she gestures to the chubby girl, "and Samantha, but we call her Sam."

"Do you like green eggs and ham, Sam-I-am?" Kiki says. Sam smiles shyly—obviously not up on her Dr. Seuss.

"They're my friends," Belle says, and the girls have a group hug.

"What are you making for lunch?" I ask.

"Veggie quesadillas," Sam says.

"You like that, right, Claire?" Belle asks.

"Sure do."

"And quesadillas just happen to be one of my all-time favorite meals," Kiki says.

"I don't like green peppers but I do like olives and salsa, and my older brother Robert eats my green pepper for me right off my plate, and he's going to university in the United States of America," Sam says.

"Wish I had an older brother to eat all the stuff I don't like," Kiki says. That makes them laugh.

"My brother is Jordon. He mostly likes beer," says Cicily.

"A man after my own heart," Kiki says. "Does he have a girlfriend?" This makes the girls laugh their asses off. Maya and I share a smile.

"Claire, did you know we're going to a c-concert tonight? We are," Belle says.

"Really? What concert?"

Belle looks blankly at Maya.

"The New Dreamers. A boy band from Seattle." Maya winks at Kiki and me. "They're coming to the Abbotsford Sports Centre. I thought it would be a fun night out for these young ladies."

Kiki starts singing and dancing around the kitchen, playing an air guitar. She's obviously heard of the boy band from Seattle. The three "young ladies" hold hands and jump up and down, screeching with delight.

"Belle, it's your turn to get lunch started," Maya says. "Cicily and Sam, why don't you play Jenga with Kiki in the living room."

"Jenga is the best." Kiki follows the girls into the living room.

"Could you please put a little oil in the fry pan and heat it up for the tortillas?" Maya says to Belle.

Belle pours a little too much oil into the pan but then spoons the excess into a cup. She carefully inspects the stove.

"What number do we want, Belle?" Maya asks.

"Th-three," Belle says turning the knobs on the stove. From the living room, I hear Kiki groan and the wooden blocks crash down.

"How about six, so we make sure the tortillas get nice and brown and the cheese melts."

Belle turns the knob slowly and counts to six out loud. In my whole life, I have never seen Belle near a stove, let alone watch her cook. Mom and Dad have always made the meals; even I'm rarely asked to pitch in with cooking duties. And they've always been very protective of Belle, maybe too protective. They don't even like her to cut her own meat. And now my sister is learning to cook—zooming past me in this very basic of life skills. For the first time in my life, it makes me feel like I have to catch up to Belle.

"You've come on a great day for lunch, Claire. Belle has totally aced the recipe for veggie quesadillas."

"I don't even know how to make quesadillas," I say.

"I show you," Belle says, as she puts a tortilla into the hot frying pan.

It's time for Maya to ride the bus with the three girls to their workplace. Yup, they all have a job at a workshop, building wooden crates to hold champagne bottles for a winery in the Okanagan. Maya told me they were even learning how to use power tools. Belle running around with an electric saw? Scary thought.

At their bus stop, Belle first hugs Kiki and then she and I say our goodbyes.

"I miss you, Bella-Belle." I hug her tightly.

"I m-miss you too, Claire." Belle lets go of the hug first. I'm missing her more.

Chapter 24

After we leave Belle and her friends, Kiki takes a bus to meet her mom at some shopping mall in Aldergrove, and I hop on the nearest Skytrain home.

Text bloops.

Ty: *Where are U this very moment?*

Me: *Hurtling through the air somewhere above New West*

Ty: *Meet U at Broadway*

Me: *K*

Ty is waiting at the Skytrain station. I open the van door, and hop up into the seat. I get a head rush. Still not used to moving quickly or being upright for very long.

"Hey," I say.

Before I can catch my breath, he pulls my head close and we kiss, long and deep. I feel warm inside, like I just had a bowl of hot soup. I've missed this. I've missed Ty.

"Shut your eyes," he says. "I've got a surprise."

"A surprise? What is it?"

"If I tell you, it won't be a surprise, will it? Just close your eyes and maybe your mouth, too." He laughs when I swat him. "Come here."

To add to the intrigue, he wraps a cloth around my eyes. The fabric feels velvety and smells like sweet perfume, probably one of Tessa's or Celia's scarves. "Where are you taking me?" I open my eyes under the scarf but it's completely black. The blackness takes me back to the hospital, when everything was black and I could only hear sounds and voices. I feel a bit jittery, but I don't want to spoil Ty's plans.

"Just sit back and enjoy," he says.

The van chugs forward. We turn right, the opposite direction from home. The motor rattles as it changes into high gear and sounds tinny once it picks up speed. We're now going faster. Probably on the Grandview Highway. I put my feet up on the dashboard and let my head fall back on the seat while the cool breeze blows through a crack in the window. The van turns left, which means we're heading north. I have no idea where Ty is taking me. We've never played a game like this before.

After many turns, stops, and goes, the van slows right down. There's a strong earthy smell of the forest—pine needles and dirt. Not salty sea air.

The van stops.

"Wait here," Ty says. "Don't move."

He first opens the sliding door behind my seat and rummages around. He opens my door.

"Can I take this thing off my eyes now?"

"Not yet." He grabs my elbow and helps me down from the seat. I step onto hard pavement.

"How am I supposed to see where I'm going?"

"Shhh." He puts his fingers on my lips.

We walk for a way until the pavement changes to a pebbly path under my feet. It smells fresh, like every molecule of car exhaust and industrial toxins have been vacuumed out of the air. A bird song sounds like a tin whistle. A crow squawks back. A few people chuckle as they walk by us. I resist the urge to yell, "Help, he's abducted me! Call the cops!"

We walk several more steps before Ty stops. He unties my blindfold. I blink a few times to get used to the light. There's a white sandy beach and a beautiful lake with mountains peeking through tree-covered hills.

"Are you going to tell me where we are now?"

"In front of you is White Pine Beach. And that puddle over there is Sasamat Lake. Welcome to Port Moody's best not-kept secret."

"It's so beautiful." I'm sure this place would be packed on a hot summer weekend. Heading into fall, the weather has gotten cooler and there are only a few other people on the beach.

"Sorry, but your mom said no swimming."

"How convenient for you." I laugh.

"Hey, I was going to flail around in the water and try to keep up with you. But doctor's orders. I'm not supposed to even let you dip your toes into the water."

We walk down the beach a way and Ty unloads his large

backpack. He spreads out a blanket on the white sand and fills a large plastic plate with wraps and brownies—from the cc, of course—and designer fizzy fruit drinks.

"Hungry?" he asks.

"No. Belle made me lunch. But, wow. I'm impressed." He's stepped up his game.

We lie on the blanket, our legs and fingertips touching.

"Everyone was really worried about you, you know. Some people never wake up from comas."

"Actually, I wasn't in a real coma—just heavily sedated."

"Still, it was a serious accident." He weaves his fingers with mine. I look up and follow the path of a great blue heron soaring across the sky.

"I see a dragon," pointing to a cluster of fluffy clouds.

"Do not."

"Do, too. See? There's the head—even has fire coming out its snout—and the long winding tail over there."

"You still on those trippy drugs?" he asks.

"My turn to start a story. There once was a guy named Pilot ..."

"Like an airplane pilot?"

"Yeah, and Pilot lived on the planet Zircon in the Cartwheel Galaxy."

"Cartwheel?" Ty groans.

"Guess what, genius. There just happens to be a Cartwheel Galaxy—you'd know that, too, if you didn't skip so many Physics classes. There's also Pinwheel, Tadpole, Sombrero, and Cigar galaxies, named for their shapes."

"Well, smarty underpants, I like the Cigar Galaxy better," Ty says.

"All right then—Zircon is in the *Cigar* Galaxy. Zirconians were a strange people with bristly hair, eyes too big for their heads, and the weirdest thing of all—their souls were visible bumps on their foreheads. Most souls were nice round bumps, like if you got a goose egg from a baseball to the head, but without bruising. Pilot was different from all the other Zirconians. He was an outcast and bullied at school because his soul had a hole right in the middle of it. It was like a wound that wouldn't heal. Your go."

Ty thinks for a bit. "Pilot had a pit bull named Spike who could speak Zircon as well as twenty-five other intergalactic languages. No one liked Spike, most of all

Pilot's parents, because Spike drank a twenty-six-ouncer of dark rum every day, and was addicted to green jujubes. Although he was a bad influence, Spike was the only loyal friend Pilot had. Pilot and Spike would talk about heavy stuff like interplanetary politics, black holes, and girls. Go."

My turn. "The ancients passed down a myth about a magical cave, a kind of portal that led to a parallel universe. A chosen one would be asked to journey into the unknown and explore the other dimension. Centuries went by and no Zirconian had been chosen. Then a shaman who was 265 years old hobbled into the village on Pilot's sixteenth birthday. The shaman went from door to door, searching for the chosen one, but had no luck. That is, until he knocked on Pilot's door."

Ty takes over. "Spike answered the door. 'What up?' he said. The shaman pushed past Spike and went directly to Pilot. The shaman inspected the hole in Pilot's soul and told him that was the sign of the chosen one. Only the shaman knew where the magical cave was and he would take Pilot there."

I jump in. "The shaman told Pilot it was his destiny

to leave everything and everyone behind and go through the portal into the unknown. And that he might or might not come back. Pilot, Spike, and the shaman set out on the adventure, walked for days and days—living off jujubes—climbed the tallest mountain on Zircon, and came to the mouth of the cave."

Ty says, "Before they said their goodbyes, the three of them lit a campfire and drank rum into the wee hours of the morning. Later that day, the shaman shook Pilot out of his drunken stupor and told him it was time. Pilot was very groggy and hungover at first, but soon he was able to focus on the dark entrance to the cave."

My go. "The shaman said he and Spike could only walk him so far, and it was up to Pilot to go the distance alone. So, the shaman lit a torch and led Pilot and Spike through the dark of the cave. It was ice cold in the cave and bats fluttered around their heads. After what felt like an eternity for Pilot, they came to a ledge at the end of the cave. Beyond the ledge was only blackness. The shaman told Pilot he must have faith. Pilot's knees were shaking like there was an earthquake, but he stood on the ledge with his toes hanging over. He breathed deeply then looked back at Spike. Spike nodded at him. Pilot nodded back, then jumped into the great black unknown. The end."

"What do you mean, the end?" Ty says. "What happened to Pilot?"

"What does it matter? It's still a happy ending. Pilot had faith and took the plunge. End of story."

"Not exactly a Hollywood ending."

"Hollywood endings tie everything up into a neat package. It's not reality. Life's messy. And besides, it's insulting."

"You think too much," Ty says.

I climb on top of him. "Kiss me."

He kisses me gently, as if I might break. I rest my head on his chest and can feel his heart beating. He strokes my hair while the birds sing in the tall trees.

Chapter 25

I started by peeking into the studio window, spying on my dad. He's so inspiring when he paints: his energetic movements, his bold use of color, and the contented look on his face that he's right where he should be.

After a week or so, I graduated to going into the studio by myself after school or late at night. I'd sit down on the meditation cushion and just look around. At my dad's work in progress or at my unfinished Downtown Eastside portraits. Or I'd look at the photos of you I took that day on the Lions Gate.

Another week went by and I managed to put my pencil on a blank page of my sketchbook. I closed my eyes and pretended I was the Fool in the Tarot cards, or

Pilot in the story, who leaped off a cliff. I let my pencil fly in squiggles and spirals. A day or so later, I created a dripping splotchy mess of a watercolor that kind of looked like the images from the Hubble telescope. And then I finally dipped a brush into acrylic paint and daubed it onto a blank canvas. A window inside of me opened up just a tiny crack. As the days went by, the window opened wider and wider.

Soon I was spending hours in the studio after my dad finished for the day, working on your portrait late into the night. I experimented with different colors and techniques and finally found a way to show your essence, your spirit, as I've come to know it. I made your expression mysterious—not exactly Mona Lisa mysterious—but it's hard to tell exactly what you're thinking and feeling. Over the past few months, I've seen too many photos of you wearing an ear-to-ear grin. And I've also seen photos of you in a very dark place. So much was hiding behind that beautiful smile of yours. I used bold dark blues for shading and reds and pinks for skin tone. I exaggerated the blueness of your eyes—definitely your best feature.

One night in the studio, I was getting close to finishing your portrait. I felt cool air swoosh by me and I felt some weird vibrating energy behind me. The hairs on my arms stood up straight. I was covered in goosebumps. I turned around, expecting to see you.

I agonized over the last brush strokes, but I finally finished. My dad is over-the-top impressed with the portrait I painted of you. Said I took some risks, pushed myself. He wants me to submit it to the Vancouver Art Show that's coming up next month. There's even a nice chunk of cash for the winners. But I have other plans for it.

Paul asked me what I hoped for you. It's an easier question to ask of someone who is actually alive. Like, I hope Belle is happy, living in her new group home. And I hope Ty gets accepted into the welding apprenticeship he just applied for. And I hope Kiki's remission lasts a long, long time. But you're dead. What am I supposed to hope for someone who's dead?

In one of my many conversations with Paul, I said to him, "Why don't we all just avoid suffering, commit suicide, and get it over with?"

Paul's response: "Why don't we just live?" He's all about embracing the good, the bad, and the ugly in life, and accepting there is some order to it all, even in suffering.

I'm starting to think he's right, but I'm not about to tell him that. Instead, I let him fatten me up with super scoops of ice cream, thinking he still has to convince me.

I hadn't been near the Lions Gate Bridge since my bike accident, until a day in early October. I looked around and thought how strange it was that everyone was just going about their lives—mothers pushing baby carriages, old people whizzing by on scooters, couples holding hands— right at the place where you ended your life. The shrine of wilted flowers and photos of you was no longer there, but someone had stuck a semi-deflated soccer ball in the railing near where you jumped. How perfect is that?

I took the journal out of my shoulder bag and sat down on the sidewalk with my back against the railing. For the last time, I read through every word I had written down from your cellphone: texts, messages, Instagram posts, and, of course, your suicide note. I ripped out those pages one at a time, and tore the paper into tiny pieces. I felt so peaceful watching them float down into the water. (Not really littering, since paper is organic.)

After I fed your words to the Burrard Inlet, I walked back down West Georgia Street with the canvas under my arm, and hopped on a bus for East Vancouver. As I watched the city rush by, I thought about the times I had taken this same route over the past months. When I took the bus to your funeral. When I left a note for Lauren and your mom that I had your cellphone, and then met Eddy and your other soccer teammates. And finally, when I delivered your cellphone to your family. Lauren's words are still etched in my mind, that you're a selfish bastard for making your mom suffer. She could be right. But still, I have found compassion for your suffering.

I got off the bus and walked to your house. I left the painting by the front door. I waffled at first, but then decided to sign it, so your mom and Lauren would know I'm thinking about them. I slid the soccer medal I removed (okay, stole) from your room into the mail slot. I took one long last look at your house and headed home through the soccer field.

Chapter 26

Kiki gives me a thumbs-up, and then pulls a helmet over her thin wisps of newly grown hair and fastens it under her chin. I do the same.

"Let's do this!" she yells out to me, shaking her fisted hands excitedly.

We're on Grouse Mountain, on the North Shore of Vancouver. Kiki's on one zipline platform and I'm on its twin, several feet away. Feels like we're on the very top of the world. Looking north, I see snowy peaks push their way into the sky. Far below us, downtown skyscrapers dot the waterfront. Traffic, like a parade of tiny ants, moves across the Lions Gate Bridge. The sun lights a path in the Burrard Inlet, the open ocean stretching into the distance.

Metal clangs as we're both clipped into the harnesses. The forest floor far below the platform is covered with drifts of snow. Floating ice crystals sparkle all around. When we're secured, I grab the handle in front of me.

"Ready, Kiki?" I call out.

"I was born ready!" She looks over with an enormous smile.

We're both launched off our platforms. Flying in midair. As I pick up speed, the cool wind nips at my cheeks. Kiki's whoops and hollers echo off the mountain as we soar through the treetops.

Acknowledgments

My whole-hearted gratitude goes to:

Peter Carver, my editor, who skillfully guided me to peel off the layers of the story and uncover its heart. Red Deer Press is a perfect home for this novel, and I am also thankful to Richard Dionne, Red Deer publisher, for taking on this book.

Susan Braley, Diana Cranstoun, Tricia Dower, Adrian Hill, Diana Jones, and Shannon McFerran—my writing friends, who so generously share their time and thoughtful insights, and inspiration.

Susan Mayse for being my teacher.

Barbara Campbell for arranging writing retreats for me in Vancouver while I wrote this, my first novel.

Stephen Price and my fellow participants at the 2015 Denman Island Writers Workshop. Your valuable feedback on a very early draft of this novel was greatly appreciated.

Marina MacCuspic for being my first teen reader all those years ago.

Dr. Ryan Allen and Constable Matt Rutherford (Victoria Police Department) for their professional expertise.

My family and friends who bolster me with love, encouragement, and wine!

Interview with Leanne Baugh

©Jennifer Callioux Photography

This is the first novel you wrote. Why was it important to you to tell this story?

The world can sometimes be a scary, confusing, and messy place—it must be especially so for young people who are trying to figure it all out. Although *Last Words* explores a difficult topic, I tried to bring a glimmer of light and hope into a world that can be, at times, pretty crazy.

I know this is a complicated question, but how do you go about deciding the order of the events in the story—for example, when Claire is going to meet Kiki for the first time, when Declan is going to read the last words of others who have

committed suicide, when the various scenes in the CC are going to occur—and so on?

It's been said that a writer's job is to elicit emotion. Therefore, when I plot or order the events in a novel, I strive for the greatest emotional impact.

In an earlier draft, I had Claire meet Kiki much later. But, as I rewrote the story, Kiki's character became more important to Claire and also as a foil to Will, so I had Kiki appear earlier in the story.

As for the placing of other events, I had Declan read last words of others who have committed suicide to reveal how isolated and alienated Claire felt, even among her friends that obviously cared about her. The various scenes at the CC were meant as emotional anchors for the themes in this novel.

What kind of research did you have to undertake as you wrote this story?

Before I began writing, I consumed any information I could find about suicide. Then I took a psychologist out for a coffee to discuss the trauma a person would face witnessing someone taking their own life. This was very helpful for me to mold Claire's character and the emotional journey she would go through. I also asked questions of a doctor friend of mine about the various medical issues that arise in the story. And I contacted my local police department about procedures and protocol around suicide, which guided how I wrote the first few chapters. And, of course, Google is always a writer's friend to help fill in any blanks.

Belle and Kiki are both clearly important characters in Claire's story. Why was it important to include each of them?

Both Belle and Kiki live life "out loud" and embrace life in their own ways. I see stories having layers of tension and conflict—like concentric circles. In this story, Claire's family is the core circle. I wanted to explore Claire's family life with all the tensions of sibling rivalry, but also show Claire's deep love for her sister, Belle, who is living life to the fullest.

Kiki represents the next layer in the story. Kiki is Claire's peer who understands life and death better than Ty, her boyfriend, or any of her close friends. I wanted

Kiki, who clings to life with every ounce of her being, to be a strong contrasting character to Will, who gave up on life.

Claire sometimes finds comfort in reading the poems of Emily Dickinson and in listening in on the conversations between Maggie and Archie. Why is that?

Art can be healing; it can help us explore emotions that are difficult to express. I believe art in any form, whether poetry, prose, visual art, or film, has a way of enhancing our world by increasing our self-awareness and self-reflection. It connects us to our collective humanity. I wanted Claire to be consoled by the poems of Emily Dickinson and the poetry ping pong of Archie and Maggie at the Cosmic Cow.

But art isn't always meant to be comforting. I also wanted to show how art could also stir up other emotions, like when Claire was deeply moved—even troubled—when she viewed a painting by Emily Carr.

Sometimes authors like to create fictitious communities in which to set their stories. Why was it important to you to set this in the real city of Vancouver?

My first draft of *Last Words* was set in a fictitious town. When a friend told me someone in his high school committed suicide by jumping off Vancouver's Lions Gate Bridge, I became curious. Soon after, I spent a weekend in Vancouver, walked on the bridge, and did some research about suicide in that city. That's when I decided to set my story in Vancouver. And I recently read about a group who are posting messages of hope on the Lions Gate Bridge in an effort to reach people who are contemplating suicide. This affirmed my decision to set my novel in Vancouver.

Mental health issues are becoming more and more prevalent for young people these days. Why do you think this is the case?

Even researchers haven't found definitive answers. However, some studies point to stresses on families, such as separations and financial problems.

Other research has found links between smartphone/device use and depression among youth. One study showed that young people who were on their phones five hours a day or more were 71% more likely to have at least one suicide risk factor (depression, thinking about suicide, or attempting suicide). Risk factors rose significantly after two or more hours per day of being online. What's lost when we're plugged in? According to the study, two big factors: face-to-face interaction and an adequate amount of sleep.

Although the title of the book is *Last Words* and it does focus on the effect Will's end of life has on Claire, it really is a story about life asserting itself in many different ways. Would you agree?

Yes, I absolutely agree. Who really has the last word in this story? Although Claire becomes a bit obsessed with Will's suicide note—his last words—it's the characters like Kiki, Belle, and Paul who really have the last word in the novel, by embracing the good, the bad, and the unknowns in life, and having faith in the mystery of it all.

What advice do you have for young writers who aspire to writing their own stories about difficult issues in their own lives?

Writing about difficult themes can stir up emotions, but it can also be very healing. My advice would be to uncover as many emotional layers as is comfortable, and see what comes. Most importantly, young writers should always look after themselves emotionally, and be discerning with whom they share their writing on difficult topics.

Thank you, Leanne, for all your insights.

Taking care
of yourself...

A Discussion for Reader's

Reading Claire's story may bring up all kinds of feelings, whether you have been depressed yourself, thought about hurting yourself, or are worried about someone else. That's okay, because when we feel things, it lets us know there might be something we need to do to take care of ourselves.

The first thing to know is that your feelings are real and are okay. Even if you don't know exactly what's going on and can't put words to your feelings, you should talk to someone you trust. If you have no one you feel comfortable talking to right now, then it's important to call a crisis line like KidsHelpPhone or check out a local integrated youth service in your area, like Foundry in BC and Stella's Place or a What's Up Walk-in in Toronto. Some organizations have also started offering counselling or ways to connect on digital platforms (ie. LGBT Youthline, Bean Bag Chat), to make taking the first step a bit easier.

There is a way through it.

That's what you need to remember in your lowest moments. So hold on, there is a listening ear, even if you don't know that yet.

As it goes in the Tony award winning musical *Dear Evan Hansen*, about a high school student with social anxiety:

> *Even when the dark comes crashing through*
> *When you need a friend to carry you*
> *And when you're broken on the ground*
> *You will be found*
>
> *So let the sun come streaming in*
> *'Cause you'll reach up and you'll rise again*
> *Lift your head and look around*
> *You will be found*

("You Will Be Found" from *Dear Evan Hansen*, 2015)

The facts

People talk about these being the best years of your life, but the facts are that young people struggle. There's so much going on between the ages of 12 and 25. Our bodies go through their biggest growth period at this time. Our brains are changing constantly, making us unsure of how to react or what choices to make. Our social and intellectual development—making new friends, finding new interests, questioning what we thought was true—make this time even more challenging.

And then there is the stress. People think that young adults don't have much stress but that's not true. The pressure of school, starting a new job, expectations of family and community, and feeling unsure of our abilities, can sometimes make life feel overwhelming. You are not alone in your struggle. All young adults face these challenges. Some of us find stress hard to handle and need help to deal with it. In fact young adults are more stressed out than any other age group.

More than one in five young adults struggle with their mental health, most often anxiety and depression. When we are depressed we feel isolated, lose hope, and sometimes harm ourselves. Feeling anxious is normal. It helps us to avoid danger. But when it gets in the way of our leading the life we want—when we have extreme physical and emotional responses to things—then it is no longer a useful feeling.

Suicide is the second leading cause of death for young people. Canada has the fourth highest rate of suicide for young adults in the 34 countries of The Organisation for Economic Co-operation and Development (OECD). And if you are poor, if you have experienced some sort of trauma like abuse or bullying, or if you identify as different from the majority of your peers, then you are at greater danger of experiencing mental health issues.

How to help

Research shows that talking openly to people about suicide in a safe and supportive environment does not increase your risk of committing suicide, but instead lessens it. Most people contemplating suicide need to feel hope that the emotional pain they are experiencing will lessen. One of the best ways to give them hope is to offer them some alternatives and show them we care. Whether you are a friend, a teacher, or a parent, these discussions are hard to have. Therefore it's important to look for support and resources in your community.

If you know someone who's struggling, the first thing to do is to listen. This doesn't mean you have to have all the answers. You can always say you get it but you don't know the answer and will help the person find out. Find someone to help you get some answers—like your parents, your friends, another family member, your guidance counselor, or a teacher you trust. There is a lot of information out there and people are more open to discussing mental health than ever before.

One way to detect an emerging problem is to look for behavior in your friend or child or student that doesn't make sense: an unlikely change, looking bad, being crabby or twitchy, complaining about not sleeping, drinking more, doing more drugs, eating differently, pulling away from friends, doing wild and risky things more than usual, or giving things away (when they don't usually do that)— or just plain acting differently.

Learning about mental health is essential. Just as we must learn how to take care of our bodies, so must we learn how to take of our hearts and minds. There are tons of resources online (some are listed below) and a trusted doctor or guidance counselor will also have great information. Or you could join a support group at school or in your community. Many school boards are committed to integrating education about mental health into their curriculum and teacher training (see Toronto District School Board site). This is also true of universities, many of which have growing support networks on their campuses (see the Jack Project and on-campus peer supports that often are available through student services).

If the burden of your friend's pain becomes too heavy for you to carry, you must get help for yourself and for her or him. If your friend or child or student has said "I don't think it's worth living anymore" or "Nobody cares if I'm alive or dead," take it seriously. This is a cry for help ... yes, they are seeking attention but they are seeking it because they are in terrible pain. Even if your friend has sworn you to secrecy, it's okay to break a promise to save a life.

Sometimes when a young person close to you hurts themself you feel you could have done something to prevent it. It's normal to feel that way but the thing is, you are not responsible! Sometimes the pain is too great for any of us to take it away.

If you lose someone to suicide or feel depressed yourself, remember Claire and Will's story. You may not feel exactly as they did but whatever your feelings, they are important and real.

Lift your head and look around, you will be found.

—*Jenny Carver, Executive Director,*
Stella's Place www.stellasplace.ca

Stella's Place is a Toronto-based organization that services young adults (16-29) who are at risk for suicide, self-harm, and other behaviours as a result of trauma and mental health challenges. We offer young adults a safe place, where they can talk openly about their experiences, and meet other young adults who have had similar experiences. We offer treatment to build capacity, resiliency, and skills for managing emotions and thoughts that have the potential to lead to harmful behaviors.

Stella's Place offers programming designed to address the whole person with respect to their wellness—using creativity, fitness, peer support, and skill-building clinical support to support their mental health. We also offer various levels of programming that reflect different levels of commitment, and this allows young adults to access us at different points of their recovery and readiness.

Resources

In every province, there is a Mental Health Crisis Line, hotline, health line, distress line, help line, or a suicide line that you can find online. In most provinces, you can call **2-1-1** for information about other mental health services.

Websites with resources and more information:

The new Canada Suicide Prevention Service (CSPS) by Crisis Services Canada, enables callers anywhere in Canada to access crisis support by phone, in French or English: toll-free 1-833-456-4566 Available 24/7

- KidsHelpPhone Ages 20 Years and Under in Canada 1-800-668-6868

- First Nations and Inuit Hope for Wellness 24/7 Help Line 1-855-242-3310

- Canadian Indian Residential Schools Crisis Line 1-866-925-4419

- Trans LifeLine – All Ages 1-877-330-6366

- Alberta Crisis Line – All Ages 403-266-4357

- British Columbia Crisis Line – All Ages 1-800-SUICIDE

- British Columbia Mental Health Support 310-6789

- BC211 – Referral Hotline 24/7 Dial 211

- LGBT Youthline - 1-800-268-9688

- Manitoba Crisis Line – All Ages 1-877-435-7170

- New Brunswick Crisis Line – All Ages 1-800-667-5005

- Newfoundland and Labrador Line All Ages 1-888-737-4668

- NWT All Ages 24/7 1-800-661-0844

- Nova Scotia Crisis Line – All Ages 1-888-429-8167

- Nunavut Line – All Ages 7 PM-11 PM (EST) 1-800-265-3333

- Ontario Crisis Line – All Ages 1-866-531-2600

- Ontario College and University Students 1-866-925-5454
- Prince Edward Island Crisis Line – All Ages 1-800-218-2885
- Quebec National Crisis Line – All Ages 1-866-277-3553
- Saskatchewan Crisis Line – All Ages 1-306-525-5333
- Yukon Crisis Line – All Ages 7 PM-12 AM (PST) 1-844-533-3030

More information:

For a program in your school, talk to a guidance counselor.

If you are in college or university, there will be a student counseling service and at some universities your student fees will cover counseling outside school, so look into it.

The Jack Project: http://www.thejackproject.org/

For LGBT youth: www.itgetsbetter.org

To learn more about mental health:

Mind your mind: http://www.mindyourmind.ca/

Mobilizing Minds project: www.mobilizingminds.ca

About Depression: www.depression.informedchoices.ca

Canadian Mental Health Association: http://www.cmha.ca/mental-health/your-mental-health/youth/

The Mental Health Commission of Canada: http://www.mentalhealthcommission.ca/English/issues/child-and-youth

For adults wanting to take a mental health first aid course go to: http://www.mentalhealthfirstaid.ca/EN/course/descriptions/Pages/MHFAforYouth.aspx